THE MAN WITH
THE MONEY

BY
ARLENE JAMES

MILLS & BOON®

MILLS & BOON and MILLS & BOON with the Rose Device are registered trademarks of the publisher.

First published in Great Britain 2003
Harlequin Mills & Boon Limited,
Eton House, 18-24 Paradise Road, Richmond, Surrey TW9 1SR

© Deborah Rather 2002

ISBN 0 263 17794 7

Set in Times Roman 10½ on 12 pt.
07-1103-41244

Printed and bound in Great Britain
by Antony Rowe Ltd, Chippenham, Wiltshire

Chapter One

Fifty bucks. Fifty lousy bucks. Charlene Bellamy fought the urge to shove the rumpled bills into her boss's smug, clueless face. The Dallas law firm for which she worked as an attorney was one of the wealthiest in the entire state of Texas, so she had naturally been encouraged when Pratt had promised her funds for her foster son's soccer team. She still couldn't believe that their contribution amounted to a measly fifty dollars.

It was going to take hundreds to outfit and equip sixteen underprivileged four- and five-year-olds, but when she'd pointed that out to her firm's youngest senior partner, he had blithely suggested that she refrain from performing so much pro bono work and actually try to bring in some income for the firm so they could do better by her next "little project.'' The cad knew perfectly well that her pro bono work had left her own bank account near empty. He also knew that, though protracted, her representation of the abused women's and children's shelter, her last case, had not only kept the shelter open by removing the threat of a frivolous but dangerous lawsuit, it had also garnered a great deal of positive press coverage for the firm. Unfortunately, positive press meant little at Bellows, Cartere, Dennis and Pratt, at least as compared to cold, hard cash.

What really angered Charly and turned her stomach, however, was the way Richard Pratt, a married man and her immediate supervisor, had stared at her breasts and suggested that he might make a hefty personal contribution if she was ''nice'' to him. It wasn't the first such suggestion Pratt had made, and unfortunately it wasn't likely to be the last, since her complaints to the other partners had brought her only smiles, lectures, reprimands and cleverly veiled threats, in that order. The irony of it was that the firm frequently prosecuted sexual harassment suits—most quite successfully. Yet, the good-old-boys mentality coupled with legal sagacity to let Pratt slide right under the bar needed to prosecute. The moment her employment contract expired—ten months and two days hence—Charly would be out of there. She was weary of being the token woman reluctantly admitted to the fringes of the good-old-boys club, but where she would go next she didn't know. Her reputation for being unable to resist championing the underdog didn't exactly make her a much-sought-after prospect for any firm dedicated to profitability.

A half hour later, she found herself standing outside a RuCom Electronics store, where she had more pressing matters to attend. Ponce and his little friends were counting on her. She pushed open the heavy glass door and walked through it into the shop, where her ex-husband was the branch manager. Surely he would help with some donation. A signal chimed. The muted clomp of the heels of her sensible pumps followed as she moved through stacks of computer accessories, telephones, radio-controlled model cars and stereo equipment on special sales promotion. RuCom was well-known for its rock-bottom prices and the stripped-down approach to retailing that made undercutting its competitors possible. The company was also known for its astonishing profit margins, and it was the latter that gave Charly hope, that and her ex-husband Dave's easy-going demeanor.

While Dave's level, laid-back manner made it possible for him and Charly to remain somewhat friendly after their divorce, it also added to Charly's pain over the failure of the marriage. After a single short year of wedlock, she had been stunned when Dave announced that it had been a mistake. She hadn't realized he was unhappy or that he blamed her preoccupation with work for it. While Charly had been thinking babies and how to fit a family into her schedule, David had been thinking divorce. Two years after the fact, she still smarted, not that she really thought much about Dave himself. It was

more the opportunity to fulfill her desire for children that she missed, so much that she'd begun to
investigate the possibility of adoption after Dave
left her. Foster parenthood had been a step in that
direction, and it was Charly's most fervent hope
that she would soon be allowed to adopt Ponce
Jack, the angelic five-year-old with whom she'd
shared her hectic life this past year. It was because
of Ponce that she was here.

Walking up to the counter, she looked at the mid-
dle-aged clerk who wore his standard-issue RuCom
T-shirt over a long-sleeved dress shirt and pleated
slacks. The usual RuCom retail clerk was a teenager
firmly rooted in computer geekdom. This guy
looked more like an executive.

"Can I help you?"

"Dave around? Tell him Charly's here."

The man blinked at her name, then pointed to a
posterboard sign on the counter. "Sorry, it's Retail
Staff Appreciation Day. The regular sales staff is
off today."

"Maybe I can help," said another voice, and a
tall, dark-haired man with brown eyes and a strong,
square jaw stepped into view, a clipboard in one
hand. "I'm in charge of the shop today."

A blatantly handsome man, he looked to be about
Charly's own age, early thirties. The older fellow
slid over and made room at the counter for him, an
obvious act of deference. The newcomer wore his
RuCom T-shirt with khakis, sans dress shirt, so
Charly could only assume that he pulled rank due
to actual sales experience. An odd, unfamiliar

awareness shimmered through her, which was puz-
zlingly uncomfortable. She wished David was here,
but since he wasn't, she could only consider her
options. The fees for the team had to be paid to the
soccer league tomorrow, or the team would not be
scheduled for games. If she struck out here, her
only option was to borrow against her credit card
and pay the fees herself. Might as well give this a
shot.

Smiling, she stuck out her hand. "Charlene
Michman Bellamy."

The man put down the clipboard and took her
hand in his, brown eyes sparkling. "Darren, uh,
Rudd."

"Pleased to meet you, Mr. Rudd." Charly took
her hand back and tried to relax, but a strange tingle
made her tilt her head and shift her weight. "I have
a problem I hope you can help me with. Actually,
it's sixteen four- and five-year-olds who need your
help. These are underprivileged kids who can't afford to buy their own school lunches, let alone the
cleats, balls and uniforms needed to play soccer. I
was hoping that—in exchange for advertisement, of
course—your shop could sponsor the team."

"I see."

His gaze swept over her, and she wondered just
what it was that he thought he saw. Fighting the
urge to tug down the bottom of her demure navy
business suit jacket, she pushed back her short,
wispy red hair and squared her shoulders.

"I take it that your husband is the coach?"

Charly lifted both brows at what she considered a sexist remark. "Certainly not. *I* am the coach."

His smile broadened, and he leaned forward, bracing both elbows on the countertop. "That's cool. I just assumed...I mean, it's usually the spouse who gets stuck with the fund-raising."

"Well, I don't have a spouse to stick with the fund-raising," Charly retorted, amazed by the speculative gleam in those brown eyes. She cleared her throat. "What I have is a five-year-old who desperately wants to play soccer and no team to play on unless I get this thing off the ground."

"This 'thing' being a team of underprivileged children," he clarified.

Charly nodded. "The soccer commissioner gave me a list of kids who couldn't get on teams because there weren't enough scholarships to cover their fees. I intend to see to it that those fees are covered and the kids get to play."

"Even if it means soliciting funds and coaching the team yourself," he surmised.

"Yes."

He straightened and folded his arms, asking, "Have you ever coached a soccer team before?"

She held his gaze. "No, but I've been reading a great deal and—"

"You think you can coach soccer from a book?" he interrupted skeptically.

She lifted her chin. "The proficiency level at this age is quite low, anyway. Besides, the most important thing is that they get to play."

"So you don't expect them to actually win any games."

She didn't, but she wasn't about to admit it. Some of the teams in the league were outfitted with the very finest equipment and had committed, competitive coaches with the time and skill to turn out first-rate players. Some of them handpicked their players from a pool of eager applicants desperate to get onto winning teams. Most of that occurred with the older age groups, but the commissioner had already warned her that one coach in her level with a flawless win record had put together a team of all five-year-olds which he expected to "kick serious butt."

Looking Darren Rudd right in the brown eyes— and quite enticing eyes they were with their long, black lashes and warm centers—Charly said, "Can you help me or not?"

To her surprise the older fellow butted in. "I'm afraid it's just not possible, young lady. RuCom policy—"

"*I* am in charge here," Darren Rudd interrupted mildly. The other man silenced like a tap turning off, but the look he turned on Rudd was all questions. The younger man smiled at Charly and said, "What Stevens was trying to say is that we don't usually make such donations, but since the cause is so very good, I think we can make an exception this time."

Charly closed her eyes in relief. "Thank you. This means more than you'll ever know. If you'd like to verify what I've said, you can call the soccer commissioner.''

As she spoke, Darren Rudd moved to the cash register and began punching buttons. ''Oh, I don't think that will be necessary. You look like a trustworthy sort.'' He smiled, and the cash drawer slid open. He started pulling out cash and counting it. ''Will, say, five hundred dollars take care of it?''

Five hundred! Charly nearly collapsed. It was enough to pay the fees with nearly fifty dollars left over. ''Yes!''

The older man gasped and exclaimed, ''But Mr. Ru—''

Rudd held up a hand, cutting off his subordinate in midword. ''If anyone has a problem with it, I'll replace the funds out of my own pocket, all right, Stevens?''

Stevens gulped and nodded. Rudd handed over the money to an impressed Charly. With those warm bills in her hand, she felt as if she'd met a kindred spirit, and the way he held her gaze made her wonder if perhaps she hadn't found more, but then she took a good look at him and mentally shook her head. The man was a hunk. It wasn't just those gorgeous eyes or that wavy brown-black hair, the chiseled features or even the broad shoulders and powerful build. He exuded an aura of confidence and potent masculinity that made itself felt as surely as any physical touch. He wouldn't really be interested in a woman like her. If she couldn't hold Dave's interest, she certainly couldn't hold the interest of a man like this! Oh, he flirted. Of course he would flirt. It seemed a part of his nature. He probably didn't even realize he was doing it, but even if it had been more, it was still out of the question.

"The kids will be so thrilled," she told him. "We'll have the team shirts printed up with RuCom Electronics Store 796 on the front."

"RuCom Electronics will suffice," he said, sounding amused, "and it'll save on printing costs."

She laughed. "So it will."

"By the way, what's the team name? You never said."

"Well, we haven't really decided that yet," she admitted.

"Good," he said. "I might have some ideas about that. I mean, since you'll be representing RuCom, we'll want it to be something cool, naturally."

"Oh, ah, well, the team would have to vote on it, you understand."

He shrugged. "No problem. When can we have a team meeting?"

"Uh, Thursday. We're practicing at a field over on Lovers Lane at Arroyo. We start about six."

Darren Rudd smiled. "Then I'll see you Thursday. Probably not by six, more like half past."

"No problem. You could even come after practice, about seven."

He rubbed a spot just in front of one ear and said, "We'll have to see. Now if you'll just give me a number where I can reach you..."

"Oh, yes, of course."

He plucked an ink pen from the counter and turned over a brochure touting a certain computer package. She recited all ten digits of her home phone number, knowing that Bellows, Cartere, Dennis and Pratt took a dim view of her "bleeding-heart projects." Darren Rudd jotted them down and wrote the name Charlene above them in bold block letters. "Actually," she heard herself say, "nearly everyone calls me Charly."

He hitched an eyebrow at that. "Is that a fact? Funny, you don't look like any Charlie I've ever seen." He actually winked at her then.

To her horror, she felt a blush start to rise. With her pale, golden coloring, it was impossible to hide it. "I'll, uh, see you Thursday then." Quickly she turned away, but then she turned back long enough to add, "Thank you. Thank you so much. And it's Charly, with a Y."

"Charly with a Y," he echoed, tucking his hands beneath his folded arms and nodding.

Charly got out of there as fast as her sensible pumps could carry her without knocking something over, blaming her pounding heart on her haste. It was only after she'd made it out to the sidewalk that she began to think how this must be her lucky day, after all.

Dave would never have given her five hundred dollars! Oh, he'd have given her something, certainly more than Pratt, but five hundred? Never. She laughed as she stuffed the bills into her purse. She could kiss the feet of whoever had thought up Retail

Staff Appreciation Day at RuCom Electronics. Just one thing bothered her.

Why had she told him to call her Charly? Only her family and friends called her that. Professionally, she was Charlene. Charlene was an attorney, all business. Charly was just a woman with friends and family. Charlene was a sharp, Amazonian warrior on the field of legal expertise. Charly was a much more vulnerable soul, a woman who desperately wanted a family of her own. Something told her that vulnerable was not a good thing to be when it came to dealing with Darren Rudd. He might be just some exec who'd worked his way up to the home office via outstanding performance in the retail end of the business at this point, but he was the sort of decisive, bulls-by-the-horn type. If she wasn't careful, he'd steamroll her, and this would be his and RuCom's team rather than hers and the kids'.

If she wasn't careful, she'd take his flirtatiousness seriously, and that could only lead to trouble. Maybe he would call her Charly, but when it came to Darren Rudd, she was going to have to *be* Charlene.

Darren snapped his fingers, hovering over the open cash drawer where he'd just put in some bills. "Come on, come on. I only had three hundred on me. You'll get it back, I promise."

"It's not the money," Stevens said, passing Darren two hundred in cash. "I just can't believe you, of all people, have expressively gone against company policy, policy you dictated, I might add. I knew nothing good could come of this retail staff appreciation program.''

Darren slid the bills into the cash register and closed the drawer, chuckling. ''I'll be honest with you, Stevens, having corporate staff substitute for retail associates is more about giving you stuffed shirts in your ivory tower a taste of the real business than letting the sales staff off for the day, though they do deserve it since they're the real money-makers.''

Stevens made a face. ''Point taken. But I don't see what that has to do with sponsoring a soccer team against company policy.''

''It hasn't a thing to do with it,'' Darren admitted. ''I just wanted to get to know the lady.''

Stevens rolled his eyes. ''Five hundred dollars to get to know a woman, when you've got a whole string of them dangling after you?''

''It's my five hundred bucks,'' Darren said with a shrug.

''What about the company policy?''

''My company, my policy.''

''And how long do you suppose it'll be before she figures out you're D. K. Rudell instead of simple Darren Rudd?''

Darren grinned. ''Long enough, I hope.''

Stevens shook his distinguished gray head. ''I do not understand you, sir. I have never understood you. I don't think I ever will.''

Darren laughed and clapped his vice-president of

operations on the shoulder. "Stevens, weren't you ever young and single?"

"Of course."

"Well?"

"Well what?"

"Didn't you ever run the race just for the joy of the chase?"

"I couldn't afford such indulgences," Stevens intoned dolefully.

Darren shook his head in pity, then grinned unrepentantly and crowed, "Well, I can, and I have a closetful of track shoes to prove it."

"And the notches on your bedpost, no doubt," Stevens muttered.

Darren tapped his temple with a forefinger. "The only record I need is right up here."

"Let us hope you keep it there," Stevens said with a sniff. In another life, Darren mused, Stevens had undoubtedly been an English butler. No one else could be that starchy. Still, he was a genius at corporate management. Thanks to him and his team, RuCom ran like a well-oiled machine. His only real fault was in his attitude toward the sales staff, whom Stevens and most of the other executives in the corporate office considered beneath them, when in reality they were the lifeblood of the company. Darren had instituted a yearly Retail Staff Appreciation Day as a means of giving his corporate staff a taste of real retailing, and being one who believed in leading by example, at least in his business life, he had gladly taken a turn behind the counter.

In truth, he'd thought it would be just like the old days when he'd been struggling to find his niche in a marketplace dominated by giants, but it wasn't. Too much water had gone under the bridge since he'd opened his first shop in Lubbock, fresh out of college at Texas Tech. The water had rushed under that bridge, actually, sweeping him along with it, and now he was the biggest boy in the business. Sometimes he missed the old days—but not for long. He made a mental note to ditch the Porsche and go with the Caddy when he met *Charly* on Thursday.

Charly. Odd nickname for a woman, especially one that looked like her, not that she was drop-dead gorgeous or anything. Now that he thought about it, she wasn't his usual type at all. He tended to gravitate toward the heavily, usually surgically, endowed sort. He liked long hair, blond preferably, blue eyes and stunning figures, stiletto heels and red lipstick. What was it about redheaded, shapely but unremarkable Charly that revved his engines so? It certainly wasn't the way she dressed! He'd had Sunday school teachers who dressed with more pizzazz.

Funny, he hadn't thought about that at the time. Now that he did, he was pretty sure she hadn't been wearing any makeup. Her squarish face was pretty, yes, in a wholesome fashion, her mouth pleasingly plump and dusky rose, nose short and, well, neither wide nor narrow, blunt nor pointed. Her brows were straight, short dashes of red-brown above round eyes that were definitely her best feature. An odd golden color mottled with specks of green and blue, they were rimmed with thick lashes much brighter and lighter than her brows. He'd had the strange sensation of waking up to find those eyes gazing at him from the next pillow, their red-gold lashes sparkling with morning light. He wondered what she'd be like in bed.

He always wondered what they'd be like in bed. That's what kept him moving on, what made him one of the hottest top ten bachelors in the nation, according to the press, that and the millions he had stashed away. He didn't fool himself that his appeal to the opposite sex was strictly personal, and while he was definitely not above taking advantage of the appeal of his millions, it secretly rankled, just a bit, that his luck with women had improved so phenomenally once his business had taken off. Maybe Charly was his chance to put that old hang-up to rest. Maybe that was why he'd invented a new identity for himself on the spur of the moment.

Something had told him that Charlene Michman Bellamy would run from D. K. Rudell. So he'd be Darren Rudd and let her run to him instead. It would be a new experience, and new experience, after all, was the name of the game, wasn't it? Same old same old got boring all too quickly, especially these days. Yeah, it was worth five hundred bucks and more just to see if plain Darren Rudd could pull it off.

Stevens had worried that she might be running a scam, that she might not be who she said she was or soliciting funds for anything other than her own use, but Darren didn't believe it for a minute. She was much too genuine, this Charly. She might be, in fact, the most genuine article he'd ever come across. He shook his head, wondering why that mattered, why it intrigued. But in the end, he didn't really care: the game was in play, and, as always, he intended to win.

Chapter Two

She was waiting in the parking garage, ostensibly adjusting the strap of a sandal with a four-inch-high heel, her firm rump all but exposed by the minuscule skirt of her spandex slip dress, when he slid the silver sport car into its assigned space. As he got out of the car, she straightened and feigned surprise, one long-nailed hand flying up to her chest and calling attention to the abundant cleavage exposed by the two tiny triangles which comprised the bodice of the so-called dress. Frowning, she adopted a petulant air, rippling her leonine mane with a practiced toss of her head.

"I'm glad I ran into you like this, D.K. I've been wanting to talk to you about yesterday."

He activated the antitheft device on the car by depressing a button in the tiny remote attached to his key chain and said drolly, "So you've decided to apologize for stepping out of line—way, way out of line—and making that scene yesterday."

She folded her arms beneath her ample breasts and threw out a hip, red mouth pursed in an effort to appear either hurt or repentant and managing neither, despite great inducement. Tawny Beekman had been living rent-free in a luxurious apartment two floors below the penthouse that Darren Keith Rudell called home. He'd offered it to her as a means of helping her straighten out her abysmal finances, since he owned the building, the apartment had been empty and she'd been evicted by her roommate. The couple of months' reprieve he'd initially offered had stretched to nearly a year, with Tawny tearfully declaring over and over again that she couldn't afford a decent apartment since she'd given up "dancing" for a living. She was supposedly supporting herself as a waitress, but he had his doubts. During that year she had done her best to renew their brief affair, though he had deliberately ended their very casual sexual relationship even before she'd moved into the building.

D. K. Rudell knew better than to let his casual affairs come too close. He never made passes at the women who lived in his building or worked in his employ. He never played around with married women or the family members of his friends or business acquaintances. He made certain that no woman ever spent an entire night in his bed, and he never, but never, gave any woman, save the cleaning lady and his sister, Jill, the code to his private elevator and a key to his penthouse, not even their flighty mother DeeDee.

Jill had rarely used the access he'd given her, but yesterday had been an exception. She'd been waiting for him when he'd gotten home from work, anxious to speak to him about their mother's latest folly, an investment scheme in a diamond mine located in, of all places, Missouri. Tawny had seen Jill accessing his elevator and assumed that she was a girlfriend. She'd ambushed him then just as she had today, complaining bitterly that he'd lied to her about not giving out his key to his lovers. She'd wept and exclaimed that she could satisfy his sexual needs far better than that "frumpy brunette." When he'd explained, through gritted teeth, that the woman in question was his sister, for pity's sake, Tawny had accused him of leading her on and breaking her heart. He'd left her screaming that he owed her, so he wasn't too surprised to see her here again today.

"Oh, baby," she cooed, gliding up to him, "I'm so sorry. How was I to know she was your sister?"

"You weren't," he said flatly, "because it isn't any of your business."

"I know, I know, but I can't help myself," she pouted, sliding a hand lightly over his chest. "You know I'm crazy about you, D.K. You've ruined me for every other man. I've missed our good times so much."

"But not enough to move out, I've noticed," Darren retorted dryly.

Anger flashed in Tawny's artificially green eyes

but was quickly replaced by woe. "I thought you wanted me near you."

Darren lightly placed his hand on her shoulder and pushed her away, saying, "You thought wrong." He dropped his hand and stepped back several steps, adding, "I tried to help out, but you knew the ground rules from the beginning. I've been more than generous. Now it's time for you to go."

The spigot immediately turned on. "Oh, D.K.!" she warbled, sniffing and blinking her false eyelashes. "How could you?"

He was immune by this time and just shook his head. "End of the month, Tawny. You ought to have a tidy little nest egg put aside by now. It's nearly four weeks, so you have plenty of time, but I'll even help you locate a new place if you want. Hell, I'll help you move, if that's what it takes, but one way or another you're out of here by the end of the month. Understand?"

She was sobbing openly now, her lovely shoulders shaking pitifully, her face buried in her hands. "How can you do this to me? I burn for you. You'll never know how desperately I want you to—"

"Yeah, yeah," he interrupted. "The thing is, see, I've moved on, a long time ago. It's past time for you to do the same thing."

"But I only want *you*," she insisted petulantly, reaching out for him.

He caught her arms and pushed them down. "But I *don't* want you, Tawny," he said softly but firmly. "I can't be any more blunt than that."

"But why?" she demanded, stomping a foot like an overtired child. "I know I turn you on."

Oddly enough, she didn't, not anymore. The awful truth was, in fact, that no one and nothing seemed to anymore, except... He pushed sudden thoughts of Charly Bellamy from his mind and took a good, hard look at Tawny Beekman. She was every man's fantasy, so beautiful that she was almost unreal. Actually, she was a lot unreal, from her phony nails to those surgically enhanced breasts. In that respect she was not much different from most of the women with whom he'd been involved. For some reason he found all the artifice unpalatable at the moment.

"Tawny," he said patiently, "it is so over. It has been for a long time, and it's going to stay that way. So get it out of your head that you can get me back into bed. It's not going to happen."

"Then why can't I stay?" she pleaded.

He almost laughed. Didn't she realize how transparent she was? Her great passion for him obviously had more to do with free rent than anything else. Once again, it was his money.

"You can't stay," he said bluntly, "because I'm tired of you taking advantage of me. You've had a good, long, free ride at my expense. Now it's over. Get used to it."

She didn't even try the tears this time, going straight to outrage instead. "You selfish son of a—"

"Oh, that's rich, when you're the one mooching free rent."

"You can afford it, damn you!"

"That doesn't mean you're entitled to it," Darren retorted dismissively, turning away. "Just vacate the apartment by the end of the month." He began walking toward the exit.

"You're going to pay for this, Rudell! You can't just toss me out with the trash! I'm going to get you! If it's the last thing I ever do, I'm going to get you, D.K.!"

He pulled open the heavy metal door that led to the elevator bank, walked through it and let it close solidly behind him, closing out the sound of her voice as she continued to shriek at him. Crazy woman. What did she think she could do? He was D. K. Rudell, after all, and she was a drama queen who'd hitched a free ride. Well, the ride was over. End of the line. And the instant she was off the gravy train, he meant to tear up the track behind it. From now on, his generous impulses were strictly little league, Little League soccer to be exact, if such a term applied.

As he fitted his key into the slot of his private elevator and punched in the code on the keypad below, he smiled, thinking of all those little kids running around with RuCom Electronics emblazoned on their chests—and a grateful Charlene Bellamy beaming up at him. He felt a fresh spurt of excitement as the elevator door slid open, followed swiftly by sheer relief. How long had it been, really, since he'd felt such eagerness? Pocketing his keys, he stepped into the elevator, turned and pushed the button, then leaned back against the wall and closed his eyes, imagining Charly Bellamy in his arms. His heart thumped in an unexpected fashion. Oddly poignant, it almost hurt. A strange warmth spread through him.

Slightly embarrassed, he cleared his throat and glanced up at the tiny security camera mounted in the corner of the elevator car. Every elevator, every entrance, every corridor in the building was outfitted with them. He often wondered what his security officers saw on those constantly lit monitors. Not much of a criminal nature had happened in this building, despite its proximity to the downtown area. They'd nailed a purse snatcher hanging around the front elevator bank when he'd tried to grab a tenant's handbag as the elevator door slid closed, and they'd flushed out a couple of prostitutes looking for a clean, out-of-the-way place to take their business. A pizza delivery guy had tried to walk off with a package left outside the door of one apartment on his way out of the building. Other than that, the residents themselves and their guests had to provide any entertainment for the security guys.

Darren had never asked, but he suspected that the silent, blue-jacketed guards had gotten an eyeful more than once, but never at his expense. He was too aware of being watched to misbehave in public or even in the seeming privacy of a closed elevator. It was an unpleasant fact of his life that people were always watching, and not just security guards. Even his most private moments often found their way into the press, however, so he made it a personal policy to break it off with any woman who spoke to reporters about their relationship. It didn't keep him from being duped by the occasional publicity hound, but it kept him from investing more in them than he could afford to lose.

He was a little surprised that Charly hadn't recognized him, frankly, but he was also glad. If he was very careful, she might never know who he really was. Perhaps that possibility explained his intense interest in her. Yes, that must be it. It wasn't her so much as it was the opportunity to step out of his public persona and into a normal life for a time. Normal was something that he vaguely remembered, but he was pretty sure he could pull it off. It must be like riding a bicycle; it came back to you once you climbed aboard and pushed off.

Feeling confident, he whistled as he stepped out of the elevator and into the penthouse foyer. He locked the elevator in place with a holding code, then opened the apartment, inserting the key into the slot in the wall that left his one-of-a-kind door unmarred by the obscenity of a keyhole. The massive twin slabs of polished and elaborately etched steel swung open with a satisfying hydraulic whoosh. Leaving them standing wide, Darren walked into the peaceful silence of his clean, spacious apartment, certain that he was utterly safe, completely untouchable. And alone.

The luxury sedan rocked over the rough ground and came to rest between a fifteen-year-old pickup with flaking paint and Charly's own sensible, fuel-efficient import. Watching from the sidelines, she knew who it was even before Darren Rudd squeezed out of the car in the limited space. She felt a jolt of anticipation mingled with wariness the instant before an exuberant, near-sighted munchkin in baggy jeans and T-shirt bowled her over. At the impact, she stumbled backward and sat down hard. The child landed on top of her. The next thing Charly knew, she was staring up at blue sky, wondering how it was possible to drown on dry land, for, try as she might, she could not pull oxygen into her lungs.

Suddenly the weight on her chest lifted away, and fresh, fortifying air rushed in. Then a number of faces came into view, most of them small and worried, one of them handsome and rather amused. Small, grubby hands patted her shoulders and head.

"Miss Charly! Miss Charly!"

Ponce shoved his way through the mob of children and fell on his knees at her side, his big black eyes revealing his fear. Curls bobbing, he leaned over her, the angelic features of his face striking her anew with sheer awe. He was a Michelangelo sculpture with café au lait skin and a froth of light, reddish brown curls that must surely hide a halo.

"Mommy!"

Charly fought up onto both elbows and found a smile for him, her heart swelling with love. "I'm okay, sweetie."

"Just had the wind knocked out of her, I think," Darren Rudd said. Charly switched her gaze to him just as he let go of the child he'd scooped off her.

The boy pushed his thick, too-wide glasses far-
ther up the bridge of his nose. They slid right down
again, and Charly made a mental note to buy the
kid an elastic sport band to hold them in place.
"I'm sorry, Ms. Charly."

"That's okay, Calvin. No harm done. I was just
about to call a break, anyway." She sat up, and
Darren Rudd offered her a hand, which she clasped
without actually looking at him. He hauled her to
her feet with athletic ease. Keeping her face averted
so he couldn't see her blush, she swiped at the
surely grass-stained seat of her gray shorts, pushed
up the sleeves of her white sweatshirt and addressed
her team. "Guys, this is Mr. Rudd. He represents
our sponsor, RuCom Electronics."

"Do you have one a' them remote cars?" asked
the tallest player, Kental, his black face shining.

"Uh, I have one in my office," Darren answered
after a moment.

"Man, them remote cars is cool," Kental said to
the dark-haired little girl next to him.

"Juan gots one," she crowed, referring to her
older brother.

"Uh-uh. The kind I mean costs a whole bunch."

"Mama bought it at the RuCom store!" Maria
insisted.

"Did not!"

"Did, too!"

"Kental, Maria," Charly interrupted firmly, one
hand idly massaging her sore abdomen, "we're not
here to discuss our toys. We have important matters
to decide. We have to have a name for our team,

and Mr. Rudd has come to help us decide on one.
Now I'm open to suggestions. Anyone have any
ideas?''

The kids all looked at one another. Some
shrugged. Others shook their heads. Then someone
suggested, ''Electrics! How 'bout the Electrics?''

''It's elec*tronics,* goofy,'' Ponce explained.
''RuCom Electronics, like computers and stuff.''

''The Co'puters!'' someone else cried.

''How about the Comets?'' Darren suggested
mildly. ''The RuCom Comets.''

The kids looked at one another in question and
confusion. ''What's a comet?'' asked Sarah, pushing stringy blond hair from her eyes. Sarah was
missing a tooth, and Charly was convinced that no
four-year-old lost a tooth to natural causes, but
Sarah clammed up whenever Charly asked what
had happened.

Charly bent down to bring her face closer to
Sarah's, smoothed a hand over her none-too-clean
hair and explained, ''It's like a shooting star, honey,
a big fireball that streaks across the sky. It's real
fast and real hot.''

Kental nodded approval at Ponce, who nodded
back. Calvin swaggered, thumped his chest and
said, ''Shootin' star.'' Maria giggled, and Sarah
smiled her gap-toothed smile. Murmurs of ''cool''
and ''sweet'' went from one little mouth to another.

''So what do you think?'' Darren asked. ''Is it
the Comets, or does someone have another suggestion?''

''Show of hands,'' Charly directed. ''Everyone

gets to vote. In favor of calling our team the Comets, raise your hand. Against it, keep your hands down.'' About twenty little hands went up, some voting twice. "The Comets it is," Charly announced with a clap of her hands. The kids cheered as she turned to Darren Rudd. He was even more handsome than she remembered. The dark hair waving back from his forehead and temples called attention to those deeply set brown eyes. His angular jaw and chin bore the shadow of a beard that glinted rusty brown in the waning sunlight.

"I'll let the commissioner know tonight,'' she told him. "Thanks for coming by, but you don't have to hang around. I'm sure you have better things to do.''

He shrugged. "Nope, not really.'' He smiled, and his gaze scanned speculatively down her body. Heat blossomed instantly in embarrassing places.

Quickly turning away, she clapped her hands at the children. "Okay, back on the field! Back on the field!'' The kids ran to obey, bouncing off one another in the process. "Ponce, will you get the ball, please?''

Ponce ran down the field and gathered up the single soccer ball while Charly attempted to set up a shooting drill. She wasn't entirely sure what the objective was beyond connecting foot with ball, but she figured if they could accomplish that much, it would be an improvement. They seemed to have better luck kicking one another than the ball. She tried not to think of Darren Rudd watching with folded arms from the sideline as she placed the ball and directed Maria, who always seemed to manage to be first in line, to take a short run and boot the ball. She spent several minutes after that comforting the child, who had managed only to kick herself off her feet and land flat on her back, bouncing her little skull off the hard ground.

When the first parents began to show up to retrieve their children, some walking from a nearby public housing sector and past several other soccer fields, Charly had accomplished little with the team and was somehow exhausted in the bargain. It was like herding geese. Their attention spans were shorter than she had realized, Ponce being the obvious exception, and while she worked with one, the others naturally scattered in pairs and trios to chase and tussle, draw in the dirt and even throw it. Charly was too busy to even think about Darren Rudd—until she turned, an arm draped about Ponce's small, narrow shoulders, and headed toward the sideline.

There he stood, talking to Kental and his mother, one large hand on Kental's shoulder. The boy smiled up at him, rapture on his thin face. Kental's mother shook Rudd's hand, then turned away, tugging her son after her. Kental skipped happily, literally clicking his heels together at one point. One of his shoes flew off, and the pair stopped so he could pull it back on. Charly had noticed that his canvas shoes, though worn, were too large for him, but whether they were purchased that way in hopes that he wouldn't outgrow them too soon or were inadequate hand-me-downs, she couldn't say. Deliberately pushing Darren Rudd from her mind, she began mentally reviewing the practice.

One thing was certain: she needed some help. Corralling sixteen little ones in an open field was an impossibility for a lone adult. Actually teaching them anything was another issue entirely. She wondered which of the parents she should ask first. None of them was likely to be of assistance. They all either had other children to be supervised or were working late shifts or second jobs. At least one of them didn't even speak English. Still, she felt that she should ask them first. After that, she would ask the soccer commissioner for help, and if that failed she'd start haranguing her friends. Someone had to be willing to pitch in.

Darren slid his hands into the pockets of his chinos and waited patiently for Charly and her son to join him, well satisfied with what he'd seen that day. Charly was so far out of her league that she'd have little choice but to accept his help. He was actually looking forward to it. "Helping" her coach the team would be like killing two birds with one stone. Not only would it afford him the perfect opportunity to get next to Charly, literally, but it ought to be fun. The kids were certainly eager, and she definitely had not overstated the needs of the children. Quite the opposite, in fact. Five hundred bucks obviously wasn't going to address all the needs. He was already making a lengthy mental list of what they were going to need, including a whistle for the coach. He wondered if she realized how many times—and how ineffectually—she had snapped her fingers or clapped her hands for attention today. More than that, however, he wondered about Ponce, or rather, Ponce's father.

As soon as Ponce had called her Mommy, Darren had remembered that she'd mentioned having a five-year-old. It simply hadn't registered at the time, perhaps because he'd been too intent on learning her marital status. He'd never dated a ''mommy'' before, not that he was dating one now, not yet. The fact that she had a child didn't bother him particularly. He liked kids. He doted on his nephew. Still, he couldn't help wondering about Ponce's dad, though. He must be an exceptionally handsome man, because Ponce was one of the most beautiful children Darren had ever seen.

His own curiosity about the man puzzled him. He wondered why Charly and Ponce's father had parted and where the fellow was now. Could she still be in love with him? The need to know was like a splinter under the skin, not particularly painful but enough of a nuisance to constantly remind you that it was there. He resisted the urge to pick at it as she stopped beside him and lifted a forearm to wipe her forehead with the sleeve of her sweatshirt. The action left her damp bangs standing on end.

Darren felt a definite tug in his groin. What was it about her? The woman should have been completely unappealing. Her athletic shoes and even her socks were filthy. Her shorts were stretched out and baggy, not to mention grass-stained. In spite of the cool, early-spring air, perspiration had soaked her shirt in spots and left her hair plastered to her head, what wasn't sticking up. She wore no cosmetics, and a spattering of freckles was even now rising across the bridge of her nose. His palms itched to strip her where she stood. Instead he smiled down at Ponce.

"You were a big help to your mom out there today."

"Absolutely," Charly agreed, squeezing the boy's shoulders. "And speaking of help, could you grab the ball and the cups for me, honey?"

Ponce nodded and moved away with a glance in Darren's direction. Darren hoped he wasn't going to have trouble from that quarter. The kid was giving off hostile vibes. Probably wanted his parents back together. Darren put aside that issue and said, "I'm afraid you're going to need more help than the boy can give you, however."

She wrinkled her nose. "I'll speak to the soccer commissioner about it tonight."

Something told him to tread softly, so he said only, "Well, if you can't get anyone else, I might be able to give you an evening or two a week."

She gaped at him. "Really?"

"If you can't get anyone else," he said, shrugging. She smiled, and her whole face lit up. She wasn't beautiful, even now, but she was dazzling. He gulped and played his next card. "I, um, can see that the five hundred isn't going to take care of all the team needs."

"The fees took most of it," she admitted with a grimace, "but we'll make do."

"I don't see the point in that," he said lightly. "Tell you what, why don't we do a little shopping, figure out how much more is needed?"

She considered briefly, then nodded. "Okay, I'll check around and let you know."

He smiled and suggested mildly, "It'll go faster if we just take care of it together. When can you go?"

She looked off into the distance, and he knew that she was considering the wisdom of spending time with him. He let her consider, and finally she said, "I'll have to let you know."

"How about tomorrow?" he pressed gently. "You busy tomorrow afternoon? I'll meet you at Sports World. I hear they have the best prices." He fished a piece of paper from his polo shirt pocket and added, "I got the kids' shoe sizes as they came off the field, all but Ponce's."

She was staring at him now. "Shoe sizes?"

"They can't play in what they've got," he pointed out. "One little girl was out there in sandals."

Charly pushed a hand through her hair, leaving it in wild disarray, and his heart literally thumped. What *was* it? "I know," she said, "but sponsors usually just provide jerseys and a few balls."

"You want them to be able to compete, don't you? The other teams will have cleats and real uniforms. As they are representatives of RuCom, we want them to look as good as everyone else."

She stared at him a little longer, and then those unusual golden eyes warmed. "That's wonderful!"

Pure satisfaction flashed over him, but he shrugged it aside, saying, "It's just good business, really."

"I don't care what it is," she told him bluntly. "All I care about is what it'll do for those kids."

"So are you free tomorrow afternoon or not?"

She bit her lip and then nodded. "I'll arrange for my grandmother to pick up Ponce from day school. How's four?"

It was early, actually, but he nodded, already planning how he could stretch shopping into dinner. "I'll be waiting out in front of the store. You do know where it is, don't you?"

"Behind the mall," she said, naming a popular shopping spot in Plano.

"That's the one. You can give me Ponce's shoe size then."

"Oh, that's not necessary," she said. "I'll take care of Ponce. You just worry about the rest of the team."

He just smiled and tucked the list back into his pocket. They'd see about that. He wanted her obligated to him, but his every instinct warned him to go easy. Unlike most of the women he knew, Charly Bellamy was not looking for a man. Well, she'd found one, anyway. All that remained to be seen was what she was going to do with him. He had some very definite ideas about that, but Charly would have to think they were her ideas first. He could wait. Then, when the moment came, he'd make his move. Something told him it would be worth it. What he didn't truly understand then was that Charly was going to define a whole new category in his catalog of conquests.

Chapter Three

Charly depressed the lock and slammed the car door, mentally girding herself for her next encounter with Darren Rudd, who, true to his word, was waiting even now on the sidewalk in front of the Sports World megastore. Tucking her handbag beneath her arm, she turned and strode smartly toward him, every step testing the narrow width of her coral-pink, knee-length skirt. The matching short, boxy, collarless jacket, which she wore open over a simple white, square-necked shell, made the outfit suitable for both the office and early spring, but she was well aware that it was also one of her more flattering suits, and she chided herself now for having chosen it.

Attractive as Darren Rudd was, she had no business getting involved in romantic entanglements, especially not now. With her application to adopt Ponce at a sensitive place in the process, she wanted nothing to detract or even *seem* to detract from her commitment as a mother. Mostly, however, it was Ponce's antipathy toward men in general. No, the last thing she needed just now was a man in her life. While a husband would have been a definite aid, a boyfriend would not. Besides, she was no good at the romantic stuff. Other things always seemed to get in the way. David had proved that.

Still, if she was going to get involved again, she could do worse than a man like Darren Rudd. He seemed to have a genuine heart for those less privileged than himself, and that, in Charly's experience, was extremely rare. It was just a shame they hadn't met at another time. On the other hand, maybe not. Without Ponce and his future to worry about, she knew that she'd have taken a stab at a relationship with Darren Rudd—and likely have gotten her heart broken in the process.

Smiling because he was smiling at her, she stepped up onto the sidewalk and offered him her hand from sheer force of habit. Instead of shaking it, he clasped it and pulled her toward the building, saying, "Right on time. Can't remember the last woman I knew who got where she was going when she said she was going to."

"You're hanging with the wrong crowd then," she told him coolly, reclaiming her hand. "All the women I know are as punctual and professional as any man."

He slid her a sharp glance and stepped aside as

the door swung open. "What is it exactly that you do, Charly?"

"I'm an attorney," she said crisply, and left him standing with his mouth ajar. Satisfaction curved her lips into a tight smile. He was back beside her within steps.

"I think you're right," he said. "Definitely the wrong crowd."

Charly laughed. She couldn't help it. "Where do you want to start?"

"Let's start at the top and work our way down," he suggested, leading the way toward the jerseys.

It was not the simple shopping expedition that Charly had expected. For one thing, he seemed determined to spend a lot more money than she thought necessary. He insisted on choosing practice uniforms as well as game uniforms in the previously chosen colors of yellow and blue: jerseys, shorts, socks, elbow and shin guards, even shoes. They argued over whether or not she was going to pay for Ponce's gear.

"It's not fair for Ponce to pay when the other kids are getting a free ride," he pointed out.

"The other kids can't afford to pay."

"That's beside the point. You're doing enough by volunteering your time."

"I don't see it that way."

He smiled and tapped her on the end of the nose with the tip of his forefinger. "I don't think that argument would hold up in a court of law, and it certainly doesn't with me. Now give over. Coach."

She sighed, knowing when she was beaten. "Are you sure you're not an attorney?"

"Not even close."

"What is it that you do for RuCom, anyway?"

He seemed to pause, but then he smiled and quipped, "Not nearly enough according to some. Actually, I'm overseeing an educational program at the moment. Few of these corporate types possess any inkling what the average sales clerk does. They see the whole business from the paper and report end. No practical knowledge at all. I've made it my mission to change that."

"So Sales Staff Appreciation Day was your brainchild," she guessed.

"Guilty as charged."

"Is it working?"

"We'll see. We're rotating corporate staff in and out of the various stores around the country. So far the reports have been mixed, but all in all, I think we'll gain a new appreciation for what our front line is actually doing."

"I think it's brilliant," she told him baldly, and watched in surprise as his eyes darkened almost to black.

"Do you?" he murmured, stepping closer. "That's nice." He lifted a hand and very lightly ran the tip of a finger along the arch of her cheekbone. "Thanks."

She found it very difficult to breathe. Until that moment she had half believed that it was her imagination, but now she knew without doubt that he was coming on to her. The pleasure of it swept over her in a glad rush, but the next instant she thought of Ponce and automatically stepped back.

"We, uh, we still have to pick up some equipment," she muttered.

The brilliance of his smile, the confident, predatory gleam of it, filled her with dismaying delight. Her heart pounded, and the tiny, sparse hairs on her arms lifted as her skin came alive. Appalled, she turned on her heel and walked off in the direction of a display of soccer balls, firmly controlling the insane urge to run.

Darren watched Charly walk away, noting with extreme interest that her hips swayed in a much more seductive manner than before. She was embarrassed about it, but he was, without doubt, getting to her. This was working out even better than he'd hoped.

Following at a short distance, he walked toward the equipment section of the store, but he did not, as she obviously expected, go to the big wire bin of soccer balls offered at a special price. He knew perfectly well that the balls were probably two or three years old, the last of an unsold lot from a previous batch, which the manufacturer undoubtedly dumped on the discounter for free, or very nearly so, in exchange for a sizable order of new balls to be sold at a good price. Such sale balls were fine for use by individuals, neighborhood play, that sort of thing. Getting booted around by sixteen kids in an hour was another matter entirely. Better to buy good game balls. Charly disagreed.

"They're little kids. They won't know the difference."

"But they *should* know the difference."

"Fine. Buy the cheap balls for practice and a couple good balls for games."

He shook his head. "Think about it. If you get them used to a lighter, softer ball in practice, then stick them in a game with a heftier, harder ball, they won't have the control they think they do. Recipe for disaster."

Sighing, she capitulated. "This thing seemed a whole lot simpler when I started it."

He chuckled. "It usually does. If it didn't, we wouldn't start half the things we do."

Her golden eyes twinkled at that. "True."

They bought a half dozen good balls, two whistles with cords attached, a practice net, goalie gear and a number of squeeze water bottles. Charly argued about the latter, saying that the kids would undoubtedly squirt each other with them.

"Of course they will," Darren admitted with a chuckle. "That's half the fun, and it is about fun, isn't it?"

She either couldn't or wouldn't argue with him then, and her eyes shone with such gratitude that he couldn't help feeling a hitch in his chest. It was half delight and pride and half guilt, something quite unfamiliar. He buried it beneath a pile of matching sweatbands and lace keepers—small, padded clips for holding tied shoe strings in place. When the purchase was totaled, Charly gasped and began trying to put things back.

"I knew you were buying too much. We don't need sweatbands and practice uniforms or—"

He reached for her hands, trapped them with his own and looked down into her earnest face, very aware that she had gone as still as a mannequin. She was a sweet breath of fresh air, this genuine, caring woman. Other than his sister, he didn't know anyone as principled. And not even Jill would try to keep him from spending money. Then again, Jill knew that he could buy the whole store without putting the slightest dent in his bank account.

Unexpectedly guilt hit him. It fled when the pale tip of her tongue slipped from between her dusky, pink lips and laved the bottom one nervously. Pure unadulterated lust roared through him in its place. For an instant, just an instant, he fully intended to bend his head and catch that dainty pink tongue in his own mouth. She must have sensed it, seen it in his eyes, felt it sparking in the air around them, perhaps even read his mind, for she suddenly stepped back, her tongue slipping safely behind her lips again. Suddenly he realized where they were and what he had almost done. Taking himself in hand and her firmly by the shoulders, he walked her a good distance away.

"We came here to buy gear for the team. That's all I'm doing."

"But you're spending too much," she argued. "You could get in trouble with your boss."

"Let me worry about that," he said, guilt prodding him again. "The only question you have to ask yourself is do you want those kids to be able to compete or not?''

''You know I do.''

''Then let me do what I came here for.''

She worried her bottom lip with her teeth, staring up at him as if she was trying to see inside his head or put her own thoughts there. ''I just don't want to get you into trouble.''

There it came again, so strong this time that it nearly knocked him off his feet. He sighed. Who knew that guilt could pack such a wallop? Reluctantly, he gave her a piece of the truth.

''The company isn't paying for this, okay? I'm paying for this.'' He raised a hand, palm out, when she opened her mouth. ''And before you start scolding me,'' he went on, ''I can afford it. Easily. Besides, I want to do it. For the kids.''

The surprise was that he really meant it. He could already see them running around the field in their spanking-new gear, as good as any other team out there. To his delight, Charly reached up and laid her hand against his cheek, her eyes as soft as eider down.

''You're a nice man, Darren Rudd,'' she whispered, ''but are you *sure* you can afford to spend so much?''

For answer, he pulled a roll of bills from his pocket and began counting them off. When he had counted off enough to pay for the purchase, he lifted it in one hand and the remainder in the other. ''I was prepared to spend almost twice as much, okay?''

She stared at the bills, switching her gaze from one hand to the other. Her eyes narrowed. "What are you, vice president of the company or something?"

He chuckled. "Nope." It was the truth. "But I am a substantial stock holder." True again.

She sighed and said, "I'm in the wrong business."

He just grinned. "Come on. I really want to do this." Turning, he led the way back to the checkout counter. She followed him somewhat reluctantly, as if torn between letting him spend so much and wanting all that gear for the kids. He paid, with no further argument from her, and the cashier called up two male clerks to help them all carry the many bags out to her car. They stuffed the trunk of her small sedan, then filled the back floorboard and seat.

Darren tipped the clerks and stood beside the car with her until both of the young men walked away. Only then did he turn a smile on her and suggest, quite casually and quite confidently, "Why don't we get some dinner? I'm sure hungry."

She smiled and, to his shock, said quite firmly, "No, thank you."

For a moment all he could do was blink at her. Then he remembered to smile again. "Aw, come on. You must be hungry, too."

"Sorry," she said with a faintly apologetic shake of her head.

He didn't know what to say. Finally he came up with, "A drink then."

"I don't drink alcohol."

"Coffee? A soft drink?"

She shook her head to both and opened her car door. "Thank you so much for your generosity. The kids will be thrilled."

"But...I thought you liked me," he blurted.

"I do," she answered simply. "The first game is a week from Monday afternoon at 5:15, if you're interested. We play at Quadrangle Park on Arapaho."

Lost in the confusion of her refusal, he just stared at her.

"Well, goodbye," she said brightly, and with that she got into her car and drove away.

He couldn't believe it. He stood there with his mouth open, watching as her car navigated the parking lot. Finally he understood that he had been rejected. Period. Hot embarrassment rushed upward from his chest. He brought his hands to his hips and shook his head.

All this for nothing!

The thought was so lowering, so deflating, so unexpectedly insulting that he didn't know what to do with it. No one, no woman, certainly, ever said no to D. K. Rudell! Darren Rudd, on the other hand, had just had his hat handed to him in no uncertain terms, and he didn't like it. He didn't like it one bit. Why, he asked himself, had she said no? She hadn't even made a good excuse!

At least, he consoled himself, the kids had all that great new gear. He really wanted to see them enjoying it, and yet he recoiled instinctively from

the idea of attending that game—or of going any-
where near Charlene Bellamy again. His own re-
action angered him. He had never in his life
avoided anyone—not even Tawny!—but this
looked like a pretty good time to start.

And yet, during that next week, he couldn't help
wondering how the team—and Charly—were doing. Had she found someone to help her coach,
someone who actually knew what he or she was
doing? Had the gear made any difference in the
team? Were they learning to work together, to actually kick and pass the ball?

On Thursday he waffled between showing up at
practice and making a date with some delicious and
very willing piece of arm candy. He couldn't think
of anyone with whom he wanted to go out, however, and he couldn't quite make himself face
Charly. Instead, he showed up unannounced at his
sister's and hung around for dinner—if macaroni
and cheese, peas, green beans and wieners could be
called dinner by anyone more discriminating than
his three-year-old nephew, Cory.

Cory always lifted his spirits, though. Confident
in the love of his parents, he pretty much ordered
Jill's household to his own liking, and he was so
darn cute about it that it was impossible to do anything but grin and go along. So instead of watching
a basketball game with his brother-in-law, Jared,
Darren found himself being driven over by a palm-
size dump truck powered by a small, determined
hand. In his role as highway, he had to lie perfectly

still on the floor and rely on Jared for game commentary.

Jared had not missed his calling by engineering heating and cooling systems for commercial buildings. He was not a frustrated sports announcer waiting to be discovered. Darren went home refreshed, nevertheless, and sometime during the night he woke to the conviction that he had not gotten where he was by backing down from personal challenges. Now that he thought about it, she had made a point of inviting him to that game on Monday. Perhaps the lady was not as flatly unwilling as she had seemed. He drifted back to sleep smiling, and on Monday he left the office before five for the first time in memory.

Quadrangle Park was a far cry from the team's normal practice field, but Darren had no trouble locating his yellow-and-blue Comets. There were a few parents on the Comets end of the single bandstand, and Charly seemed unaware when he joined them. The next forty-five minutes were agonizing as the Comets lost three to zip, though no score was announced. The kids simply didn't know what they were doing. Those who had the potential to be real competitors simply kicked the ball anytime it came near them—without the slightest concern for which direction it would go. Others were so out of the game that they were digging holes and playing tag in the backfield, and that included the goalie. Most were just confused, standing aside with big eyes and fingers in their mouths while the other team went after the ball.

Darren found himself shouting instructions from the bleachers. Charly finally glanced his way and began parroting his instructions to the team. By the end of it, a few of the kids were really beginning to get into the game. It was Kental who best perceived the ignominy of their debut, however. As soon as the game was called, he ran to the sidelines along with his teammates and loudly announced, "Man, we suck!"

Charly quietly reprimanded him for his language before sending them out to shake the hands of the opposing team. Afterward, however, she scheduled two practices during the next week. Then oranges and apples were passed out, and the kids were crowded into two minivans and a decrepit sedan belonging to various parents, all except Ponce who busily helped his mother gather their equipment: balls, clipboard and forms, goalie gear, ice chest, first-aid kit. Darren stuffed his hands into his jean pockets and wandered over to Charly.

"Tough luck," he said.

She snorted. "Luck had nothing to do with it." Sighing, she pushed a hand through her hair and admitted, "I just don't know what to do about it."

"Maybe you could use a little help," he suggested blandly.

"I asked around. All the dads have to work. The moms are as clueless as I am. The commissioner says they're short of volunteers this year."

Darren rubbed the back of his neck with his open palm, wondering why he was doing this. "Maybe I could help."

She looked away and admitted almost reluctantly, "You do seem to know something about the game."

"I'm no expert."

"Compared to me you are," she said, looking him square in the eye.

He just shrugged, and after a moment she said, "You'd have to speak to the commissioner, go through a background check."

He grinned. "I think I can manage that."

She smiled at him gratefully. "They looked great in their new uniforms, anyway."

"Yeah, they did." He rocked back on his heels, quite pleased.

It was then that Ponce tugged on his mother's hand. Looking up at her with that angelic face he asked plaintively, "Can we go now?"

"I have to turn in my game report first," she said apologetically, taking up the clipboard and heading for midfield and the young official waiting there with the other team coach.

Darren watched her walk away, noting the blue jeans and pale yellow T-shirt she wore. He made a mental note to get a couple of coaches' uniforms. Then again, maybe just jerseys. It would be a shame to lose those jeans. She really had quite a nice shape to her, a very natural, very real, very womanly shape.

"Whatcha lookin' at?"

"Huh?" Surprised, Darren glanced down at the boy. "Oh, uh, I was just thinking that we ought to get your mom a team jersey, too."

Ponce looked at his mother, then at Darren, and in that moment man and boy understood each other perfectly. The kid might as well have shouted for Darren to keep his hands off Charly. Darren was asking himself how a kid like Ponce had come to the correct—and very adult—conclusion, when Charly returned.

"Can we go now?" Ponce pleaded. "I'm hungry."

"Sure, baby. How does pizza sound for dinner?"

Ponce wrinkled his nose. "Too long. I want chicken bits and fries."

Charly smiled and nodded in resignation. Ponce ran toward the car. Charly looked at Darren and said, "I can't seem to break him of the fast-food habit."

"Yeah, I know what you mean," Darren told her. "My nephew eats what he eats and that's it. At the moment it's macaroni and cheese for every meal. His mom compromises by adding vegetables."

She cocked her head. "How old is your nephew?"

"Three. Cute kid. Spoiled rotten."

Ponce tooted the car horn, and she turned in that direction, saying, "I've gotta go."

He hadn't realized that he was hoping she'd invite him along until it was obvious she wasn't going to. "Sure."

"See you tomorrow."

"Tomorrow?" he echoed.

"I thought you heard. Practices are on Tuesday and Thursday now."

"Oh, right."

"I'll call the commissioner in the morning."

"Nah, I'll take care of it," he said, knowing perfectly well that Darren Rudd would never pass a background check because he didn't exist. D. K. Rudell, on the other hand, would be no problem, providing the commissioner was willing to listen to reason concerning the need for anonymity. "I'll have the commissioner call you with the okay."

"All right."

The horn blared again.

"Kid's starving," Darren joked, and she nodded. "See ya."

"You bet," he said as she jogged toward the car.

Alone, he watched them leave, aware of an odd yearning. He couldn't have said what he yearned for, but he felt as if he was somehow on the outside looking in, like he was the only kid not invited to the birthday party. What was it about Charly Bellamy that did this to him? On a scale of one to ten, rating the women with whom he'd been, Charly was no more than a seven, surely. Yet, on her, seven seemed like a perfect number.

He left even more confused than he had been, but content for the moment with the knowledge that he would be seeing her again the next evening.

Charly's heart pounded as she guided the car through the busy parking area, mindful of the children darting about heedlessly. It was perfectly ju-

venile, the way she reacted to him, and if she had
a brain in her head she wouldn't have agreed to let
him help her coach the team.

Help her? Now that was a laugh. What she knew
about soccer couldn't fill a thimble, as evidenced
by the team's performance on the field today. When
she came right down to it, she really had no choice.
The kids needed someone with more know-how
than she possessed, and Darren was the only likely
source on the immediate horizon. It would be selfish of her to turn away his help just because he
made her feel like a giggly adolescent mooning
over her first boyfriend. Besides, he had made a
significant financial investment in the team.

She would feel better about it if she didn't so
look forward to seeing him on a regular basis. Oh,
this was dangerous. Darren Rudd was dangerous.
And generous, concerned, caring...

Dangerous. Definitely dangerous. She'd a hard
time walking away from him just now. The impulse
to invite him to join them had been very nearly
overwhelming. Ponce's little voice intruded into her
thoughts. It was as if he'd read her mind.

"D'you like that guy?"

Charly felt heat blossom in her chest, but she
kept her gestures and reply cool and measured.
Reaching up, she adjusted her rearview mirror so
she could see Ponce in the back seat. He sat safely
belted into place on the passenger side.

"Mr. Rudd?" She shrugged lightly. "Yeah, sure.
Why do you ask?"

Ponce looked out the window, turning his face away. "I dunno."

"Don't you like him?"

"I dunno."

"He's been very generous in helping the team."

"Uh-huh."

She brought the car to a stop. "Does something about him bother you, Ponce?"

The boy looked down at his hands. Sometimes he looked so sad that it just broke her heart. "He likes you."

"And that bothers you, Ponce? Why?"

"My mom," he said quietly, "my *other* mom, when a guy liked her, she'd go off and I wouldn't see her sometimes for lotsa, lotsa days."

Charly put the car in park and twisted in her seat to look at him directly. "Ponce," she said, "that's not going to happen again. That's never going to happen again." She reached out a hand to him, her heart in her throat, and said, "Don't you know how long I've waited for you? Since before you were born, Ponce, I've waited for you to come into my life. Being your mom is more important to me than anything else in the world." He took her hand, beaming a smile so bright that it brought tears to her eyes. "Okay?" she asked.

"'Kay," he said.

A car tooted its horn behind them. Charly twisted around to face forward again, checked the traffic and pulled out onto the street.

"Let's get you some dinner," she said happily. Her chest ached. It simply didn't have room enough for all the love she felt for this beautiful little boy. Not Darren Rudd or any man stood a chance against him, and his fears were enough reason for her to keep Darren at a distance. She simply ignored the pang of disappointment that she felt at the thought.

Chapter Four

"Calvin, honey, no! Wait until— Calvin!" Charly sighed as the boy charged forward to get at the ball, which Kental then shot right past him.

Darren blew his whistle, and, predictably, play came to an immediate halt, albeit with much groaning and slinging of limbs. They just wanted to bump and tussle and chase after the ball, these kids. The finer points were completely lost on them, not that they weren't capable of learning, provided the teacher was patient, friendly and prone to much repetition. Darren walked out onto the field and laid a companionable hand on Calvin's shoulder.

"Hey, buddy, you're leaving your position again. I know you want to kick the ball, and that's good, but if you stay back in place and wait, you can kick the ball *and* be the hero. On the other hand, if you go up to kick it and they get by you, then you're

the goat, because there's nothing and no one between them and the goal. See?''

Calvin nodded, pushed his glasses back up onto
his face and asked, ''What's the goat?''

''In this case the goat is the person everyone will
say messed up.''

''Oh.'' The boy made a face, and his glasses
promptly fell down again. Making a mental note to
get the kid an elastic band to hold his glasses in
place, Darren repositioned the boy's sweatband so
that it covered the ear pieces of his too-wide
glasses, lending them a bit more stability.

That done, Darren picked up the ball, jogged
back to the sideline and motioned Sarah over. He
handed her the ball, backed away and blew his
whistle again. Just as they'd practiced, she lifted the
ball over her head with both hands and lofted it
onto the field. Things pretty much broke down from
there, but at least Calvin stayed in his place. Darren
felt Charly at his elbow.

''They listen to you,'' she muttered.

''They'd listen to you, too, if you'd remember to
use this.'' Turning slightly, he flicked the whistle
hanging from a cord around her neck. Charly gri-
maced.

''I keep forgetting the darn thing.''

As she spoke, Kental shoved down Ponce in a
frenzy to get to the ball. Charly had the previously
forgotten whistle between her teeth and was heading onto the field before Darren could react in any
way. The shrill bleat brought everyone to an instant
halt once again. By the time Charly reached them,
the other kids had gathered around and Ponce was

sitting up, one hand going to the back of his head. His face was red and twisted, but he wasn't crying.

"You shoved!" he accused.

"You got in my way!" Kental exclaimed, defending himself.

Darren jogged up in time to hear Charly ask Ponce, "Does your head hurt? Do you want to sit down, honey?"

Ponce shook his head and got to his feet. Suddenly he lunged at Kental and knocked him flat, crying, "See how you like it!"

"Ponce!" Charly gasped.

"Hey, hey, hey!" Darren said, stepping in to prevent any further aggression. "Come on, now. We're all teammates."

"I want you both to apologize," Charly instructed sternly.

Kental rose to a sitting position, dusted off his hands and spluttered, "*I* didn't shove *you* on purpose."

Ponce fisted his hands. "Did, too!"

"That's enough," Darren said sharply. Crouching, he looked from one to the other of them. "Soccer is a contact sport. That means players are naturally going to bump into each other, but shoving is against the rules. If you start shoving, the refs will call fouls and give free shots to the other team." He looked at Kental and said pointedly, "Good players aren't bullies. They're smart. They hook a foot in and slip that ball out of the pack. A smart player is better than a fast one or even a good shooter." Turning to Ponce he remarked, "If another player shoves or elbows a smart player, he keeps his cool. That way, his team gets the advantage. If he retaliates, shoves back, both players are likely to wind up sitting on the bench and neither team gets the advantage.'' Pushing up to his full height, he laid a hand on each of their shoulders and added, ''Soccer is a team sport, but if you keep making each other mad, how are you going to play together, and then what happens to the team?''

Both looked shamefaced by now. Charly bent forward and added her voice to Darren's. ''Now, let's have those apologies, or do you want to spend the rest of practice watching from the sidelines?''

Ponce was the first to mutter, ''Sorry.''

Kental echoed Ponce. ''Sorry.''

Charly rubbed both boys' heads and smiled. ''Okay. Let's all take a water break and rest a few minutes.''

The children ran together toward the ice chest, a mob of little bodies jostling together. Darren smiled. They were cute as all get-out, a jumble of drooping socks, flopping ponytails, sweatbands and baggy uniforms. More important, they were actually improving. Their next opposing team was in for a surprise. He was pleased in a way he'd never expected. Charly, however, was troubled.

''I can't believe Ponce did that.''

Darren looked around in surprise. ''It's no big deal. All little boys suffer spurts of aggression, no matter how sweet they look.''

''He doesn't just look sweet,'' Charly retorted. ''He *is* sweet. Normally.''

''Well, sure he is,'' Darren said, ''even more than the rest of them.''

Charly brightened. "He really is the dearest little boy."

"And one of our best players," Darren said, wondering if he'd found the key to Charly's heart. Funny, since learning that she was the boy's foster mom, he'd expected her to be less certain than most moms of her little one's superiority. Instead, she was every bit as bad as Jill, if not worse.

"Do you really think so?"

Fortunately, he didn't have to lie to her. "Absolutely. He and Kental are definitely the stars on this team."

She literally glowed. "Well, I thought so, but I wasn't sure, you know, that it wasn't just personal prejudice."

He chuckled and said very casually, "Maybe I'm a little prejudiced myself, but I still think he's one of the best, if not the best, player on the team."

The way she looked at him then warmed his blood. He lifted a hand and skimmed it down her arm, watching her breath hitch. Electricity danced in the air around them. She was not immune. No matter why she wouldn't go out with him, she was attracted sexually. He stepped closer, and suddenly a small body was shoving between them.

"Mama, can we have the oranges now?"

Charly stepped back and looked down at her foster son. "Not now, honey. After practice."

The way he said "'Kay" with such easy acceptance told Darren that the boy had not really expected any other answer or particularly cared what answer he got, for that matter. His one purpose in asking had been to separate Charly from Darren. It wasn't the first time, and Darren knew that he could do nothing but back off and concede the match.

He went to the sideline and got himself a drink, then sat with the kids, teasing and laughing with them, all except Ponce who stayed by his mother's side. After about five minutes Darren got up, blew his whistle and motioned the team back onto the field, but even as he turned his mind back to the task at hand, he couldn't help thinking that Ponce was both the way to Charly's heart and the greatest obstacle. He didn't stop to consider why getting Charly to fall for him was important. It just was. Picking up the ball, Darren tossed it to Ponce and jogged to the sideline, where he clapped his hands and pointed out positions to the kids. When the goalie—a quiet, chubby girl named Tulia who had proven to be both patient and quick—was in place, Darren nodded at Ponce. Lifting the ball over his head, the boy waited for Darren to blow the whistle. Then he threw it over everyone's head to the center of the field.

"Good job, Ponce," Darren called, clapping his hands. Though shameless pandering, it was, thankfully, true. A glance in Charly's direction showed him that it was also working. Ponce might not particularly appreciate the praise, but she did. Her smile was as warm as her eyes. Darren turned his attention back to the field, satisfied. For the moment.

She was more nervous now than she had been at the first game. The kids were so pumped, so sure they were going to win this one. They were definitely improved, but it had only been a week, for pity's sake, two practices. No one could reasonably expect them to actually win, and yet Darren seemed to. He certainly had them believing it, anyway. Charly couldn't help worrying that they might all be bitterly disappointed if they didn't live up to their own expectations.

As she walked back from the center of the field, where she and the other ''head coach'' had met briefly with the ref to turn in official rosters for the game, she couldn't help noticing that Darren was on his knees in front of the kids, speaking. Despite swinging legs and busy hands, they listened raptly. Then, as Charly drew near, they tumbled off the bench to gather around Darren and stack their hands on top of his. Bending, Charly added her own to the mix, then pumped with the rest of them and shouted, ''Comets!''

Darren stood back, and she began making the assignments. ''Tulia, we have that goal.'' She pointed, and the girl ran onto the field.

''Stay cool out there,'' Darren called, cupping his hands around his mouth. ''Stay alert.''

''We get the kickoff,'' Charly went on. ''Kental, you take it. Ponce, remember to pass that ball. Defense, play your spots and try not to let them get that ball past you to the goal.''

''And remember what I told you,'' Darren added, bending to bring his face close to theirs. ''We're a team. Maybe we're not all buddies off the field, but on it we're best friends, and we work together.''

Kental and Ponce looked at each other and nodded. Sarah slid her arm through Maria's.

"Let's get to it," Charly said, sending them out onto the field with a wave of her arm.

"Go get 'em, Comets!" Darren yelled, clapping his hands.

The ref waited until everyone on both teams was in position, or as close to position as they were going to get, before he blew his whistle and backed away from the ball. Kental took a run and booted it. Everyone on the sidelines immediately started shouting encouragement and instruction. Both teams mobbed the ball, which, after some confusing seconds, rolled slowly free of the wriggling mass of kicking legs. Ponce immediately picked up on it. Charly screamed for all she was worth as he kicked it down the field—in the wrong direction.

"The other way! The other way! Turn it around!"

He finally figured it out, went around the ball and kicked it in the opposite direction.

"Pass it to Kental!" Darren shouted. "Pass it to Kental!"

Ponce paused to look to the sideline, then kicked the ball to Kental, who was dancing in place, his tongue hanging out one side of his mouth as he concentrated on making the play. When the ball got to him, he turned and punted it down the field. Maria was there and kicked it out of bounds. So it went for half an hour before anyone so much as took a shot on goal. That someone, though, was Ponce, and when the ball actually flew past the other team's goalie and into the net, Charly could not contain her joy.

"He did it! He made a goal! He did it!"

Darren reached out a hand to pound her on the back in congratulations, and suddenly she knew exactly who she had to thank for her son's moment of triumph. Gratitude flooded her, and she threw her arms around his neck, hopping up and down at the same time. Darren put his head back and laughed, even as his long, strong arms wrapped around her waist, trapping her against him. Then he simply lifted his chin and kissed her.

It was just a smack, really, a quick, full-mouth meeting of lips, and yet, heat instantly exploded throughout her body and she became abruptly aware of him. The bulk of his muscles surprised her. She felt and identified the contours of his hard chest and thighs, the way his pelvic bones jutted slightly from a flat belly. His arms contained a ropy strength that was not in the least frightening, but it was his hands that she most felt, the wide, long-fingered weight of them seemed to burn right through her clothing. Those hands knew exactly what they were about, how to touch a woman, hold her. They displayed no tentativeness, no surprise, just a warm, easy familiarity. One of them cupped the knob of her hip just below her waist. The other splayed across her ribs, the thumb resting beneath her arm against the side of her breast. It was enough to lock the air in her lungs and stop her heart with a pronounced thud.

"I told you he was the best," Darren said, grinning ear to ear.

For an instant, just a split second, Charly had no idea about what or whom he was speaking. Then it hit her. Ponce! The soccer game! Then it, or rather *he,* literally hit her, from the back, his small arms clamping around her legs.

"Mama! I won! I won!"

Charly twisted out of Darren's arms and stooped to scoop up Ponce.

"You scored! Yeah! That's wonderful! I'm so proud of you."

"We won the game!" Ponce announced proudly, lifting his arms over his head. Darren chuckled and patted the boy's head, reaching from behind Charly to do so.

"Not quite, pal. We still have fifteen minutes to play. But you did real good. You scored the first goal for the game and the team. Better get back out there now. The ref's holding up the game for you."

Ponce's eyebrows rose sharply. Then he kicked out of Charly's embrace and ran back onto the field. As soon as both feet were within bounds, the ref blew his whistle, and the other team threw in the ball. Like Ponce, the rest of the Comets seemed to think they had the thing won. By the time Darren got them back into the game, clapping and calling out to them, the other team had taken the ball down the field and taken a shot on goal, which Tulia easily stopped. They were not so lucky the next time when, in the last seconds of the game, the other team tied it up.

The kids didn't know the difference. They ran to the sidelines laughing and asking happily, "Did we win?"

"Not quite," Darren told them with a huge smile, "but we didn't lose, either."

"It's a tie," Charly explained. "One to one. Oh, I'm so proud of you all!"

"Bet we win next time!" Kental proclaimed excitedly.

"Practice hard and we just might," Darren said. "Now who wants ice cream?"

They all started hopping up and down, yelling, "I do! I do!"

"Well, let's get loaded up then," he said, sweeping up the ball bag. The kids, all except Ponce, started running toward the parking lot. "Slow down! Watch the cars!" Darren waved over the two mothers who had driven the kids, and they hurried to shepherd the kids safely to the vans. Ponce stayed next to Charly. Darren thrust the ball bag at him. "If you grab our balls, I'll load up the water cooler while your mom takes care of the paperwork."

Ponce hesitated, but the moment Charly nudged him, he grabbed the bag and shot off to look for their balls. Darren smiled down into Charly's eyes. "They're as happy as if they had won."

"And you did it," she told him honestly.

He lifted a hand and skimmed his fingertips over her cheekbone. Suddenly she was hot again, despite the brisk March breeze. It seeped from her pores, radiated from her bones, pooled in private places, turned her muscles to jelly. "We did it. Seems we're darn good together."

She looked into those deep-brown eyes and felt the hairs lift on the back of her neck. This man was so dangerous! Much more dangerous than she had even realized, and somehow she seemed to be losing the will to resist him. But that couldn't happen. It mustn't happen. She backed up a step, and the world broadened again. Turning, she picked up the clipboard from the end of the bench and walked out onto the field. With every step she grew stronger, firmer, more in control. That was the answer then, distance. Somehow she had to keep her distance from Darren Rudd. Somehow.

It rained and turned colder that week. Charly called Darren at the number he had given her to let him know that practice was canceled, leaving a message on his answering machine. He called her back that evening. She was wiping down the kitchen counter, just finishing the after-dinner cleanup, and Ponce had gone to his room to play with his miniature cars. He had set up an elaborate roadway system with plastic building blocks and could push his cars along it, crashing them at intersections, for hours. It was a completely foreign type of play to Charly, but her grandmother assured her that it was utterly normal and very "boy." Expecting that it was her grandmother calling now—they spoke several times every day—Charly reached for the telephone receiver mounted on the kitchen wall.

"Hello."

"Hello, there, coach."

"Darren."

"So we're off for tomorrow, huh?" he asked in a chatty manner.

"That's why I called," she replied dryly. "The practice field is a bog at the moment."

"Wonder if we could find someplace else, some-thing indoors, maybe," he mused.

She rolled her eyes, chuckling. "That's not nec-essary. Everybody's in the same boat. Chances are this week's game will be canceled, too."

"Guess there's nothing to be done about it, then," he said resignedly. "Need help calling the kids?"

"I've already taken care of it."

"So what are you and Ponce going to do tomor-row evening instead? How about a movie? That new kid flick is supposed to be pretty good."

Charly blinked at her gray-green kitchen coun-tertop. He was asking them out. Not her, well, not *just* her this time, but them, her *and* Ponce. The temptation to say yes was rich. Instead, she closed her eyes and told a blatant lie. "Uh, we've already made plans to have dinner with my grandmother."

Darren didn't miss a beat. "Your grandmother? Hey, you're lucky. I never knew my grandparents, and my dad passed on when I was a boy, so it's just me, my sister and our crazy mom now. How about you? Any other family besides your grand-mother?"

"Uh, not around here," Charly said, processing the knowledge of his father's early death and that "crazy mom" remark. "My parents live in Flor-ida."

"No brothers or sisters?"

"Nope. Only child."

"I'd have hated that," he said bluntly. "Even when my little sister was a pain, I enjoyed being the big brother. Always wanted a little brother, too, truth be told, but Mom never had any more. Babies, that is. Husbands, yes. Babies, no.''

"I always wanted siblings," Charly heard herself saying, "but my parents never intended to have more than one child. Their work was too important, and they thought they'd be spreading themselves too thin. They're supposed to be retired now, but as far as I can tell that just means they don't have offices to go to."

"Why kind of work do they do?"

"Oh, they're both attorneys."

He chuckled. "Naturally."

"Mom specializes in environmental concerns, and Dad is an expert in OSHA litigation."

"Sounds interesting. What is it that you special-ize in?"

"Lost causes mainly," she quipped. "My firm's in general practice, and frankly, I'm the token fe-male. They shuttle me all the weird ones. Right now I'm working on an antidefamation suit involving two Mexican restaurants."

"Somehow I don't see you spending your life litigating whose burrito gets bragging rights," he quipped.

She grinned and admitted, "Okay, so I strike a blow for the good guys once in a while. According to my boss I'm the office bleeding heart—and about as useful."

"Hey," Darren said, "if I needed a hotshot at-torney in my corner, I'd want it to be you."

Charly could not suppress the flash of satisfaction that produced. "Well, the next time some Tex-Mex chef sues you for saying his tamales are made with armadillo instead of pork, I'm your girl," she quipped.

The atmosphere changed instantly. The guy wasn't even in the room, and everything shifted somehow. "I'd like that," he said, his voice gone husky and soft, "if you were my girl."

For a moment Charly couldn't get her breath. She felt his arms around her again, the solid warmth of his body, the pressure of his lips. She put one hand over the microphone in the end of the telephone receiver and gulped. This shouldn't be so hard, not with so much at stake. She dropped her hand and said lightly, "Anytime you need a lawyer, just call."

He sighed and changed the subject. "Tell me about your grandmother. Sounds like you're close."

The tension eased, and Charly gratefully launched into a long monologue about the woman who had essentially raised her, Delphina Michman, now nearing eighty and painfully arthritic but still vibrant and so very wise. Darren occasionally interrupted to ask pertinent questions or make remarks that clearly demonstrated his interest. Delphina kept Ponce every day after kindergarten, just as she had Charly at that age, and Ponce called her Granna Pheldina. They laughed over that.

Then Darren said, "Man, I wish I'd had someone like her when I was growing up. Jill and I pretty much fended for ourselves. Mom was always more interested in the men who were interested in her, and believe me, with her looks, there has never been any shortage of those. Even now her social life's busier than mine, but at least she's stopped marrying everyone who asks her. I know a couple good divorce lawyers who've made a living off her.''

Charly noted that though he spoke somewhat disparagingly of the woman, his voice contained a good deal of fondness, even a tinge of pride. ''That must've been rough for you,'' she murmured.

''In a way. On the other hand, I turned out pretty self-sufficient, and Jill has made it her life's ambition to be as different from Mom as she can be. The result is that she's a darn good mother and wife.''

''I can tell you're proud of her.''

''Oh, yeah. Jill's the best. She keeps me sane, you know, her and her family. When the world gets crazy, as it will, I drop by Jill's and let her fuss over me for a while, or I'll just play with my nephew. These days I'm the road over which he prefers to drive his toy cars.''

Charly laughed. ''What is it with you boys and your cars?''

''What, are you kidding? A car is freedom, power. It's a cool measure. The cooler the car, the cooler the guy.''

''Silly me, I thought it was transportation, something else to be taken care of.''

''You sound just like my sister now.''

''Go figure.''

''No, a lot of women consider a car an accessory, like a cute purse or something.''

She laughed. Suddenly it occurred to her that they were becoming friends. That was nice, real nice—and dangerous. She cleared her throat. "Listen, I have to go. It's time for Ponce's bath."

"So early?"

"We start our days early around here. If I don't get him down by eight, I won't have time to get myself ready for tomorrow."

"What do you think our chances are for having a practice on Thursday?"

"Slim. That field is a sea of mud after a good rain."

"Guess our best hope is that they'll call the game, then," he said with a sigh. "That means it'll be a whole week before I can see you again. Unless I can convince you to go out with me."

Charly bit her lip. It was so hard to say no, but somehow she got the words out. "That's not a good idea, Darren. Ponce takes up all of my free time, and he comes first with me."

"I understand," he said, "so why don't the three of us—"

"That's not a good idea, either," she interrupted. "You see, Ponce has a problem with men. His biological mother often left him with strangers for days at a time and even alone once that we know of, so she could go off with a man. He never knew his father, and apparently her boyfriends weren't very nice to him."

"All the more reason for him to get to know a stand-up kind of guy, don't you think?"

"He has a male therapist," she said. "I'm afraid for now that's all we have time for."

"And what about you?" Darren asked softly. "When are you going to make time for you?"

"When Ponce is really, truly mine," she said. "When the papers are signed and the judge says I'm his legal mother."

Silence, and then Darren mused, "Maybe you're more like my sister than I realized."

"Well, thank you, since you seem to think so highly of her."

"Yeah," he muttered pensively, "I do."

"I have to go now," Charly said softly. "I'll call you to let you know when we can practice next."

"Call anytime," he said.

"Goodbye, Darren."

She hung up the phone without waiting for him to return her farewell. For a moment she couldn't help wondering what might have been and if it could still be at some future date. But, no, it was best not to even go there. No matter how much she might want to.

Chapter Five

When the elevator door opened, Tawny whirled around and smiled, clearly pretending that she hadn't known Darren's private elevator was on its way down. Quickly Darren reached over and punched the first button within reach. As the doors began sliding closed again, Tawny's expression of innocent surprise altered to one of anger. Darren shook his head. He wasn't going to play this scene again. Twice in the past week, she'd managed to "bump into" him. Both times they'd wound up arguing, but no matter what she said or did, he was not going to give in. He wanted her out of the apartment, out of the building, out of his life.

As the elevator rose again, he thought about how much his life, how much he, had changed lately. He still couldn't quite understand it. All he knew was that it had to do with Charly Bellamy. She wasn't like all the other women in whom he'd been interested. She wasn't like his mother. No, Charly was more like his sister. Except that Charly was determined to keep him at arm's length. And it hurt. It hurt more than seemed possible, certainly more than was reasonable. Some part of him felt...empty because Charly wanted nothing to do with him— nothing personal, anyway.

Yet, he wasn't ready to cut his losses and move on. It would have been the smart thing to do, and he knew it, but he just couldn't. He could not back away from her. Maybe if he hung around, not pressing her, just as a friend, once Ponce was formally adopted, she would be more open. He wiped a hand across his forehead, fully aware that no one who knew him would ever believe he was even thinking this way.

The elevator door opened on the eighth floor. Darren strode out and turned a corner. The next one brought him to a full bank of elevators. He punched the down button, waited, then got on an elevator already containing a young couple who had recently moved into number 84. He had the distinct impression that they'd been kissing. Security guys must've gotten a real eyeful. Darren decided they were due a friendly warning, a rather oblique warning; he didn't want to embarrass them.

"Hi. How you doin'?" he asked, poking the garage button. They were going to the first floor, which was at street level.

The man glanced at the woman before answering Darren. "Good. You?"

"Not bad. Off to coach a Little League soccer team."

"That explains the jersey."

Darren glanced down at himself, smiling. "Yeah, well, I like the kids if not the clothes."

The man glanced at the woman again, and the words just tumbled out of him, his happiness obvious. "We're expecting a baby."

"Hey! Congratulations!" Darren shook his hand. It was the perfect segue. "You'll really appreciate all of this building's security features, then, like the cameras in all the elevators and public areas." He pointed to the tiny aperture containing the lens.

The woman reached for the man's hand. "Is it always on?"

"Twenty-four hours a day."

The man jingled change in his slacks pockets. "They, uh, they don't have audio, do they? I mean, they can't hear what we say, can they?"

Darren smiled apologetically. "I don't think they actually listen, not usually, I mean. There are about two dozen setups, and while you might be able to monitor that many screens, you wouldn't want to listen to that many speakers. That would be too confusing. But the audio is recorded and listened to at times."

The man and woman traded looks. "Why would they listen to the audio, do you think?" she asked.

"Oh, if they saw a crime taking place, maybe."

They both relaxed visibly. "How long would

they keep something like that on tape?'' the man wanted to know.

''The tapes recycle themselves every forty-two days unless pulled.''

The relief was palpable. Darren couldn't help smiling. ''Listen,'' he said brightly, ''have you checked out the rooftop garden?''

''Not since we moved in,'' the man said, ''but it's one of the reasons we picked this place. We work downtown and didn't want to fight the traffic every day.''

''This way we'll be close by if the baby should need us for any reason.''

''We already have a nanny lined up.''

''The garden will be a safe, beautiful place for our little one to play.''

''Most of the buildings around here don't want children.''

''Or they're not right for children.''

''This one's perfect,'' they said in unison.

Darren laughed. ''I'm glad. I'm really glad.'' The elevator had come to a halt, and the door slid open as he spoke. Darren stood back to let the pair exit in front of him. The man held the woman's arm as if she were made of spun glass and might break just by exiting the elevator. ''Nice talking to you,'' Darren said as they flipped him waves and moved away.

He folded his arms, still smiling, as the doors slid closed again and the elevator continued on its way. They didn't have enough kids in this building. The designers had told him not to plan with kids in mind, that no one would want to raise a family downtown, but instinct had told him otherwise. He wouldn't mind raising a kid of his own down here someday. His thoughts abruptly slid back to Charly—and Ponce. For a moment everything just seemed to stop, his heart for one thing, the elevator for another, the whole world, in fact. Then he realized that the elevator really had stopped and that the doors were standing open.

Shaking his head, he walked out into the garage and headed toward his car, his spirits lifting with every step. In his jeans pocket he carried an elastic band designed for athletes who wore glasses.

"I think it's a grand idea," Darren announced, much to Charly's chagrin.

"That's because you don't have to build the thing," she muttered.

"Well, of course I'll help build it," he said, bringing his hands to his hips. "We'll all help build it. That's why it's called a team float."

The kids applauded and began hopping up and down. Most of them didn't have the slightest notion what a float or neighborhood pride was, but everyone understood the concept of a parade. The mother who had proposed the idea beamed, her smile a startling white in her dark face.

"All the kids should get to ride in the parade," she said excitedly, "in their game uniforms." The kids cheered and hopped up and down some more. "I was thinking we might get a trailer, you know, and put a goal on one end of it and make it like a comet going into the net.''

"Sounds good to me," Darren said to the woman. "Think you could draw up a design for us?''

"No, not me," she said quickly.

"I can!" Maria insisted, raising her hand.

"I can, too," Kental vowed.

"Tell you what," Darren said, "everyone who wants to should draw a picture of what he or she thinks our float ought to look like. Then Coach Charly and I will choose the one we think will work best, and I'll take it to a designer I know and have a plan made of it.''

"And where will we build this amazing float?" Charly asked pointedly.

Darren rubbed his chin. "We could probably do it in the garage of my apartment building downtown.''

Charly looked doubtful. The mother who had brought them the idea of entering a float in the Neighborhood Pride Parade bit her lip and suggested, "Maybe we could do it in the park.''

"And if it rains?" Darren asked gently.

She looked downcast. "There's an empty warehouse down by the old grocery on Tempest and Sandy Lane," she suggested. "I don't think anyone would mind if we used that.''

Charly remembered that there were several liquor stores and bars in the area, too, and shook her head, resignedly coming to a reluctant decision. "We'll build it in my garage.''

"And that would be where?" Darren asked.

"Hillcrest and Samples, off Forrest Lane. It's the house I grew up in. Belongs to my parents, who live most of the year in Florida now."

No one had to say that Hillcrest was one of the better streets in Dallas proper or that it was a heck of a lot closer and easier to reach than the downtown area. Darren nodded his approval and looked expectantly to the kids and the few parents who had gathered around after practice. Everyone smiled and nodded in agreement.

Darren slapped his hands together with obvious relish. "Okay. Drawings are due at practice day after tomorrow. I'll see about getting us a trailer and speak to my designer. Coach Charly can take a look at her schedule and let us know when we can work on our float. We've got just ten days to get it ready. Any questions?" No one spoke, so Darren leaned down and laid his hand palm up, saying, "All right, then."

As the kids scampered off, Darren turned to Charly with a broad smile.

"This ought to be fun."

"Yeah," she agreed weakly.

Fun. That was exactly what troubled her. Everything Darren Rudd did was fun—innocent, disarming fun. And she was the only one who couldn't seem to just relax and enjoy it. Even Ponce seemed able to enjoy the moment, so long as Darren's attention wasn't too pointedly focused on her. She, on the other hand, often felt as if she was sliding down a particularly slippery slope—right into Darren Rudd's waiting arms. She tried to tell herself that she was being foolish. No man could make any woman fall in love with him against her will. She was quite sure that wasn't even his intention! Yet, somehow it seemed to be happening, and she just didn't know what to do about it.

Some fun. Oh, yeah, like hugging a boa constrictor that had picked you out as lunch. The problem was that she didn't think she would mind Darren Rudd wrapping himself around her.

Charly saw the last of the team members off and wandered through the house, a hand idly massaging the back of her neck. She had pretty much written off the float when she'd seen the pictures that the kids had produced at practice just over a week ago. Not one of them was workable in her opinion. For one thing the concept of limited space was lost on the average five-year-old mind. Besides that, she didn't see how she and Darren and one or two moms could put together anything more than a couple of posters in the time they would have to work. Yet, despite her misgivings, the thing out in her garage was really taking shape.

Somehow Darren had turned the batch of wild scribblings that the kids had brought them into a solid plan that seemed to convince each and every member of the team that his or her idea had won out. A day later a large, flat-bed trailer and a heap of supplies had appeared in her driveway. The next evening Darren had shown up with about half the kids and a stack of pizzas.

In truth it was Darren and one or two of the parents who were doing all of the work. Charly spent most of her time corralling the kids, who more often than not wound up in Ponce's bedroom, the den or the backyard. To her delight, Ponce, Kental and Calvin had become fast friends. As a result, Ponce seemed so happy that it made her want to cry. He was no longer the solemn little boy who had broken her heart when she'd first met him. Lately he talked a mile a minute.

A sound from the garage caught her attention. Had someone stayed behind? She'd put the garage door down earlier, so it couldn't be someone who'd walked in off the street. Quickly she moved through the kitchen and down the short back hall to the door that opened into the garage. Very cautiously she pushed the door open and stuck her head into the garage. The overhead light was on, but she couldn't remember whether or not she'd turned it off earlier. Something metal plinked against the garage floor then, and Charly jumped a yard. The next instant a voice grumbled about substandard bolts, and she realized who her remaining guest was.

Crouching at the front of the trailer, she bent her head near the floor and looked beneath the trailer bed. "I thought you left."

Darren turned his head toward her, arms raised. "I did, but after I dropped off everyone I came back to fix this stupid ramp cage."

The fixture that was supposed to hold the ramp in place when it was stored beneath the trailer had fallen down earlier in the evening, and Darren had said then that he would fix it. Charly just hadn't expected him to fix it tonight.

"Can't it wait?" she asked with barely concealed irritation.

"I've got it now," he said with a grunt, cranking his wrist. Laying his wrench on his flat stomach, he shoved himself out from under the trailer, saying, "Just needed a new nut. The threads were worn on the old one. I picked one up while I was out." Sitting up, he wiped his hands on the thighs of his jeans and smiled at her. "Couldn't have the thing falling down during the parade, now could we?"

"No, indeed," she agreed, pushing up to her feet. He twisted, grabbed the side rail on the trailer and hauled himself up, tucking the wrench into his back pocket.

"Besides, I've always believed that the best time to do something is right now. Otherwise, something else comes up and you forget. This was a safety issue. Had to be done now."

She couldn't argue with that, so she folded her arms and asked, "When did you slip back in?"

"When you were walking Kental out front to meet his father. I thought you saw me."

She shook her head. He looked down, then turned suddenly toward the trailer. "I ought to have a word with the fellow I bought this thing from. That ramp cage is supposed to be welded in place."

Charly had to close her mouth in order to say, "You *bought* this trailer?"

He seemed surprised at her rather censorial tone.

"Well, sure. We couldn't very well nail stuff to a rented one."

"Don't you think you're taking this a little too far? It's Little League soccer, for pity's sake. How can you possibly afford this on a regular salary?"

"I never said my salary was my only source of income," he told her quietly.

Charly blinked at that, feeling rather ridiculous. It wasn't any of her business how the man spent his money or where it came from!

He pretended to study the float, finally announcing, "I predict that we'll have the best-looking float in the parade."

She nodded and rubbed her arms.

"I wanted the kids to have something they could really be proud of," he said softly.

Now she felt like a heel. After swallowing she said, "I didn't mean to sound critical."

He grinned. "Believe me, I couldn't have bought a tenth of the pleasure for twice the cost." He looked at her then and said, "Thank you. If you hadn't walked into that particular shop on that particular day, I'd have missed all this." She laughed. She couldn't help it. "No, I mean it. You nudged me into something I'd never have done on my own."

"Oh, I don't believe that. You're much too generous, a well waiting to be tapped. Someone sometime would have engaged you in a similar project."

He shook his head. "Uh-uh. Because it wasn't the project, you know. I couldn't have cared less about kids' soccer at the time. I did it for you."

She was stunned, flabbergasted. Thrilled. It must have shown. He smiled and lifted a hand to the back of his neck, admitting, "Hasn't turned out quite how I expected. Instead of me getting next to you, the kids have gotten next to me. I really enjoy the time I spend with them. It's worth every cent I've spent." He dropped his hand and added, "But I'll admit to a certain disappointment where you're concerned."

Charly closed her eyes. "Darren, I...I don't know what to do with you."

He turned to face her. Stepping closer, he suggested silkily, "I'd be glad to make a suggestion."

Once again she laughed, but softly and without amusement. *Why now?* she cried inwardly. Why couldn't she have met him years ago, before David even? Then again, would she ever have met Ponce if she'd met Darren first? After all, it had been that ticking biological clock, the unfulfilled need to be a mother, that had driven her to apply for foster parenthood. Closing her eyes, she said, "Darren, please understand, i-if circumstances were different..."

"If Ponce was yours," he said softly, urgently, stepping very close now, "then would you..."

She looked up, her heart beating pronouncedly. "Would I what?"

"Would you let me do this?" he whispered, sliding his hand into her hair at the back of her head. She couldn't speak, her gaze trapped by his, her whole being held in some kind of thrall. He bent his head, and his mouth settled over hers as gently as a feather floating on the air. She could not keep her eyes open or prevent her body from swaying toward him. Then his arms came around her and pulled her against him, his mouth suddenly devouring hers. The world did a slow flip, turning upside down and spinning lazily in place.

Charly held on to the only thing she could find, Darren. Without even knowing that her arms had encircled him, she clutched at the back of his shirt. His feet tangled with hers, their knees knocking together. His hand slid down to her buttocks, spread across them and pressed her closer, until they stood belly to belly. The world righted itself with a clunk. Suddenly they were both exactly where they should be, the ground solid beneath their feet, bodies fitted together perfectly. She'd have laughed with sheer delight if her mouth hadn't been full of his probing tongue.

"Are y'all makin' a baby?"

Just like that, it all blew apart. What had seemed so right an instant before was suddenly revealed as a horrible mistake. Charly didn't even remember wrenching free of Darren, but somehow she was staring down at her frowning son. "Ponce!"

It was Darren who answered the boy's question. Going down on his haunches, he placed a hand on the boy's slender shoulder. "No, Ponce, we're not making a baby. Why would you think that?"

He shrugged away Darren's hand. "My old mom, she said that was how I got here, so I shouldn't complain if I saw her doing it. Then she sent me to my room."

Charly put her hands over her face. What had she done? Darren, on the other hand, said gently, "Charly and I were just kissing, Ponce. Kissing does not make babies. It sometimes leads to it, but it takes a lot more than a kiss to make a baby."

"Do you want to make a baby with my mom?" Ponce asked bluntly. Darren opened his mouth, but Charly quickly intervened.

"No one's making any babies around here, and I think you and I need to have a little talk." She made herself look to Darren, who rose silently beside her. "Good night. I—I'll call you."

His mouth flattened into a tight line, but he nodded. "All right."

"P-please don't, uh, come over o-or call until I do."

He bit his lips, and she could see that he was struggling not to argue with her, but in the end he simply nodded and began to ease away. "I'll wait to hear from you."

She couldn't look at him any longer. "Thank you."

He looked at the boy. "Good night, Ponce."

Ponce looked away, murmuring, "'Night."

He paused a moment longer before finally turning and hitting the button to lift the garage door. Darren hung his head as the door cranked up. Then he walked swiftly away. Grabbing Ponce's hand, Charly hurried over to put down the door, then turned toward the house.

"It wasn't what it seemed, Ponce," she told him softly. "I'm not going away with Darren."

"Is he coming here, then?"

"No. No, honey. He's not coming here. I mean, he's not coming here to live or anything like that."

Ponce looked up at her, his face troubled. "I'm good to you, ain't I?"

"Good to me? I—I'm not sure I understand what you mean."

"My old mom," he whispered, "said I wasn't no good to her, that she needed a man."

Charly swallowed her gasp and pulled him close, cradling his head in her palm. "Sweetie, you are the best thing that's ever happened to me. I think your old mom was all mixed up in her head. Some women think they can't be happy unless they have a man around, any man, but the truth is that unless it's the *right* man, she's better off without him. But that has nothing to do with you. A real mom puts her child first, nothing is more important to her than his well-being and happiness."

"What about a dad?" Ponce wanted to know.

"The same," Charly assured him. "A real dad just wants what's best for his son or daughter."

"I never had a dad," he said.

You've never had a mother until now, she thought. "Lots of kids only have one parent, Ponce," she told him gently. "They grow up just fine."

He nodded, and put his arms around her legs in a strong hug.

Smiling softly, she cupped his small shoulder blades and pressed him to her, but inside her heart was breaking for a little boy who had never been loved before, for the mother who had not known how to love him, the father who had thrown away his chance to do so. She would not be so foolish. She would not wish for anything that would not have brought this boy into her life. No, she wasn't sorry that she hadn't met Darren Rudd long ago, that they had not fallen in love, married and brought their own children into this world, for then she would not have reached out and found Ponce.

"I love you, son," she said quietly. "I love you."

Chapter Six

"Hi, it's Charly."

"Thank goodness," he said with a long sigh. "I was afraid I wouldn't hear from you for days and days."

Charly lowered the telephone receiver and took a deep breath. This shouldn't be so difficult. It wasn't difficult. She wouldn't let it be difficult. Lifting the receiver to her ear once more, she said smoothly, "I thought the sooner we discussed this the better for everyone concerned."

"Something tells me I'm not going to want to hear this over the telephone," he stated. "Can't we meet? Say tomorrow about six?"

Charly closed her eyes, wanting to refuse, knowing that she'd feel like a genuine heel if she did. After all, if someone in whom she was interested was going to tell her to take a hike, she'd rather it was done in person. "All right. Where should I meet you?"

"Ah, I have a place at 712 Ridge. That's not too far from you, just a block off Midway."

"A place?" she asked uncertainly.

"A commercial property. Uh, would you rather come here?"

To his apartment? "No. That's not a good idea."

"Okay. Well, do you have a suggestion, then? I just thought we'd meet in the parking lot over on Ridge, if that's all right."

"The parking lot is fine," she said quickly.

"All right. See you tomorrow, then."

"Tomorrow," she confirmed and hung up, sure she'd made a mistake, just not certain what it was.

After tomorrow, though, the ground rules would be set in stone. She'd tell him, in no uncertain terms, that if he ever kissed her or pursued her in any fashion, she would walk away and leave the team to him. In fact, she really ought to do it, anyway. He was the real coach; it was more his team than hers. Ponce would still get to play, and she wouldn't have to see Darren except on game day. She'd miss the other kids, sure, but she'd have more time to concentrate on work and other projects. It was the perfect solution. She should definitely resign as coach of the soccer team and stay away from Darren Rudd. So why did the very idea make her want to weep?

*   *   *

The small, pink brick building at 712 Ridge was surrounded by a fenced parking lot. Apparently, it was being used by a limo rental service, as the only vehicle in the secure parking lot was a long, black limousine with darkly tinted windows. Charly eased her midsize sedan through the gate and into a space. Before she even killed the engine, the right rear door opened on the limo and Darren leaned out.

"Charly," he called, waving her over. Puzzled, she got out of her car, routinely pocketed the keys and locked the doors, then walked back to the limo.

"What's going on?"

"Nothing. I thought we were going to talk."

"In a limo?"

"Why not? It's comfortable." With that he slid over. She either had to get in or walk away. She got in. He was sitting in the far corner. "Have you eaten? Because, I'm starved."

"Uh, no, but—"

"Might as well talk over dinner, then. How's Mexican? I'm in the mood for Mexican."

"Uh."

He leaned over and pushed a button on the console. "Pat, let's try Sala's."

"Yes, sir."

The limo engine rumbled to life. The door locks depressed, and they started to move. Charly whacked a hand against the leather seat. "What is going on?"

He looked mildly surprised. "Look, you don't

have to eat, if you don't want to," he said, "but I'm hungry."

"What's with the limo?" she demanded.

"I keep it parked here. It's safe, so don't worry about your car."

She couldn't believe this guy! "You *own* this limo?"

"What? You don't think I can afford it?" he asked with dry sarcasm.

Charly threw up a hand. "I don't know. I don't care!"

"If you must know," Darren said, folding his arms, "I bought it from a friend who was in the limo rental biz until he had a major heart attack. Actually, I bought the building and the lot from him, and he threw in the limo as an extra."

In other words, he had bailed the fellow out, Charly surmised, and the idea made her like him all the more. Not good. Seizing the first semiderogatory remark she could find, she mumbled, "What are you, made of money?"

He chuckled. "Flesh and bone like every other red-blooded male." He relaxed his arms and added softly, "All too human, I'm afraid."

She turned her head, gazing blindly out the window. This would be so much easier if he wasn't such a nice man. "You're making this into a *date,*" she said softly.

"Oh, no," he replied. "If this was a date, we'd both be dressed to kill and I'd be plying you with champagne."

Looking at him was pure reflex, though why was a puzzle. She already knew that he was wearing chinos and a polo shirt, just as she knew that she wore jeans, loafers and a nubby cardigan sweater over a plaid shirt, and yet she glanced down at herself, too. "That's your idea of a date?" she muttered, tugging her sweater closed in front. "Dressed to kill and champagne?"

"Sure, if you throw in dinner and dancing, concert or the theater. Why, what's yours?"

"Mexican food and Margaritas," she snapped.

He chuckled. "So forget the Margaritas." She rolled her eyes. "Look, I don't want to get dumped on an empty stomach, okay?"

"You're not getting dumped," she pointed out. "We'd have to be involved before you could get dumped."

He shrugged. "It feels like I'm getting dumped, but have it your way."

"I intend to."

He gusted a long-suffering sigh and said, "So before you shoot me down, could we talk about something else? Please?"

"That depends," she muttered. "What do you want to talk about?"

"Tell me about Ponce," he said. "It would help me to understand."

That was true. She took a deep breath and turned slightly in her seat. "He was removed from his mother's care due to neglect about a year ago. No one knows who his father is. She named six or seven men it could be, but they ruled out the three of them they could find. His grandmother is very elderly and in a nursing home. She doesn't even know she has a grandson because of advanced dementia. So far as anyone can tell, he has no other family.''

''Poor kid.''

''Not anymore,'' she said flatly, and Darren smiled at her.

''No, not anymore. Now he has you. And obviously he's suffered no permanent damage.''

''That's true in most ways,'' Charly admitted. ''So far as we can tell, his birth mother, or his 'first' mom as he calls her, didn't use drugs or drink alcohol while she was pregnant with him.''

''I'd say that's a given,'' Darren agreed. ''Ponce's way too bright and dexterous for that.''

''No, her addiction seemed to be men,'' Charly said, ''and when Ponce got in the way of that, she dumped him, sometimes on strangers, and made him feel worthless and unloved.''

''Time will take care of that,'' Darren assured her.

''That's pretty much what the counselor says.''

''Believe it,'' Darren said. ''You and time are all that boy needs.''

Charly smiled. ''From your lips to the judge's ears,'' she said. ''We have an adoption hearing scheduled in three months.'' At that moment the limo pulled up in front of a small, nondescript restaurant tucked into the corner of a strip mall.

"No judge would deny you the right to adopt that boy," Darren assured her. Then he opened the door and got out, holding down a hand for her. Charly slid across the seat and twisted to set both feet on the ground. Placing her hand in his, she allowed him to pull her up and out of the car. Darren closed the car door and escorted her toward the restaurant. The limo pulled away.

In short order, they were seated at a corner table. Chips and *salsa* appeared, and suddenly Charly was ravenous. The *salsa verde* was the best she'd ever tasted. "This is amazing," she said, pointing to the dish of green sauce.

"Mmm. They make it with avocado, lime juice and cilantro. I have the recipe, if you're interested, although I like a little more kick in mine."

"You cook?" she heard herself asking.

"I love to cook," he answered. "How about you?"

She shrugged. "Me? Mostly I love to eat, which is a good reason *not* to cook, except, of course, that I have to think of Ponce." They'd spoken of this before.

"My sister tries really hard to feed Cory properly," Darren said, "but I think kids get hung up on certain food at different ages, you know? I mean, we all like what we're comfortable with. Me, I'm comfortable with experimentation, but I remember clearly that in sixth grade I ate nothing but potato chips, French fries and canned pork and beans. You know, the kind with the little wieners in it."

She laughed, wrinkled her nose and said, "Gross."

"No, I still like them," he said. "It's just that there's so much more that I like now. The other day," he said, warming to his subject, "I had blackened rib eye with the most spectacular béarnaise sauce, and last night I grilled asparagus with pineapple and chicken chunks."

"Grilled asparagus?" she repeated.

"Spectacular," he promised, bringing thumb and forefinger together in the age-old sign for epicurean perfection. "And not long ago," he went on, "it was Hopping John."

"Hopping what?"

"Black-eyed peas and rice cooked with sausage, tomatoes and chilies. Serve it on top of corn bread with a side of greens. Oh, man."

"Stop," she laughed. "I'm already hungry. If you keep talking like that, I'll eat this whole basket of chips."

He waved that away as a lame excuse. "You can afford it."

Fortunately, the waitress arrived before she had to acknowledge the compliment. The young, dark-haired woman carried a smile of familiarity in her eyes. "Mr. Darren."

"Teresa. What's good today?"

"The cowboy tacos are *muy bueno*," she answered, "and the shrimp *coctele* is just made, very fresh."

"I heartily recommend both," Darren said to Charly.

She went for the cowboy tacos, even though the menu said that the trio of oversize tacos made with chunks of meat cooked in a chili sauce came with rice, beans, grilled vegetables, lettuce, tomato, grated cheese, sour cream and *guacamole.*

"Might as well bring a carryout box with it," she told the waitress. "I'll never eat all that."

"Make it two," Darren said, "and bring us a pitcher of that *sangria* iced tea you make. No alcohol," he added to Charly.

The tea came immediately. It was delicious, delicately flavored and not too sweet. She drank the first glass in a hurry and deliberately savored the second.

"This is one recipe I haven't gotten Sala to part with," Darren said, sipping from his own glass, "and try as I might, I can't nail it on my own."

"Mmm, honey," she mused.

He snapped his fingers. "That's it! I've been sweetening it with sugar."

"Lime juice," she went on, "strawberry, a little bit of grape."

He laughed and smacked the table with one hand. "Wait'll I tell Sala. I'll test it out in my own kitchen first, of course. Get the proportions right."

"And a little bit of peach in here," she went on, "or maybe mango."

"You're brilliant!" he told her with a laugh.

They were still discussing the ingredients of the tea when their dinner arrived.

Charly ate until she was miserable, then loaded the leftovers into the container provided for lunch the next day. Perhaps it was the quality of the food or perhaps it was merely a way to put off what she had to say. Whatever the reason, she usually exercised a little more discipline. By the time she was done, the conversation had turned to the law.

"So what do you like best about practicing law?" Darren asked.

"That's easy, problem solving. People come to me with problems. I find solutions. That's the best part."

"I never thought of it that way."

"Lots of lawyers don't think of it that way," she admitted, "but that's how I see it. My boss says that's why I don't make much money at it."

"Money isn't everything," Darren said, "unless, of course, you don't have any."

"But there is something to that old saw about finding satisfaction in your work, your life," she said intently. "Don't you think?"

He nodded. "Yeah. Yeah, I do. On the other hand, you can do a lot of good with money."

"As long as it's not a substitute for personal involvement," she insisted, and he smiled.

"That's something I'm learning now. Thanks to you."

The waitress returned then to begin removing the plates and ask how everything was.

"Excellent, as usual," Darren told her with a wink. He pulled cash out of his pocket and thrust it into her hand without even asking for the check. He got to his feet, obviously expecting no change, and Charly followed suit. Tucking the carryout container into the crook of one arm, she followed him to the door. The moment they stepped outside, the limo slid into place in front of them. How wealthy was he? she wondered. As wealthy as he was charming, apparently.

Neither, however, changed what she had to do.

He handed her down into the car, and she slid all the way across, placing the carryout container on the seat next to her. Darren slid in beside her, closed the door and reached for the intercom button.

"Back to the lot, Pat."

As the limo moved off again, he opened a small refrigeration unit tucked into the corner of the elaborate console and stowed the leftovers inside. Smiling, he said, "We should've brought Ponce. Sala makes a dish he calls Mexican Fries. It's French fries, of course, but with cheese and mild chili and ketchup that's just a little spicy. Kids seem to love—"

"It's out of the question," she interrupted gently.

He blinked, obviously taken aback. "I only meant...I know how important your son is to you, and I like Ponce. I like kids in general, but I really like Ponce."

She shook her head, touched but determined. "I've promised my son that I won't subject him to

any man. He was abused by some of his birth
mother's boyfriends, spanked, derided by them, one
apparently even locked him in a closet. He doesn't
trust men.''

"But how will he ever learn if he's never exposed to a decent guy?'' Darren asked.

''He is. His therapist is a male, and there are the
fathers of his teammates and friends.''

''And what about you?'' Darren asked softly.

''We've been through this already. My only concern is for my son.''

''I think you're making a mistake. I think Ponce
needs to be exposed to a similar situation with a
man who won't abuse him or consider him an in-
convenience, someone who really likes him.''

''That may be true,'' Charly conceded, ''but
what happens when this 'nice guy' moves on? What
does Ponce learn from that?''

For a moment Darren didn't reply. Then very
carefully he said, ''You don't know I'll move on.''

''Oh, yes, I do,'' Charly scoffed. ''I know it very
well.''

''You can't,'' he countered. ''You've no idea
who I am.'' He clamped his mouth shut, a glimmer
of frustration in his brown eyes.

''You're right. But I know me.'' She turned
away, gazing unseeingly out the window at her
side. ''You'll move on,'' she said, keeping her
voice light, unconcerned, though inside a space
seemed to open, an empty space. *Just like David.*

After a long time he muttered quietly, almost to himself, ''I'm not so sure.''

She ignored that, concentrating instead on what must be done, said. ''It doesn't matter what might or might not happen if we start seeing each other because we won't. In fact, I think it best if we see each other as little as possible, so I'm going to re-sign as head coach of the soccer team.''

''You can't do that!''

''Why not? You're the better coach. You can take them through the rest of the season.''

''I can't let you do that,'' he stated flatly. ''You're the heart of that team, Charly. Without you there would be no team.'' He shook his head. ''No, if one of us has to go, it will be me.''

''But you're the better coach.''

''That's not important. You know everything you need to.''

''Now, maybe,'' she said, ''but if not for you—''

''I won't lie to you, Charly,'' he interrupted, ''I don't *want* to give up the team. I love coaching those kids, more than I ever dreamed I would, but that's exactly what I'll do if you try to resign. I mean it, I'll walk away without even looking back before I let you quit.''

''But that's stupid!''

''Maybe, but you have my word on it. If you leave, the team dies.''

It was blackmail, pure and simple. ''That's not fair!''

''And leaving these kids in the lurch is? Just because you're attracted to me when you don't want to be, you'll walk away from them? That's fair?''

For a moment she could do nothing but gape as she felt her face turn red. It was pure pride that conjured the words, ''I never said I was attracted to you.''

He smirked at her, his gaze stating clearly that he had expected honesty of her. She gulped, knowing he was right. ''It doesn't matter,'' she murmured. ''Don't you see that I have no choice? My hands are tied in this. My son comes first, period.''

He wanted to argue. She could see that, and she was flattered. To think that a man like Darren Rudd would actually pursue her was a considerable boost to her ego, not that she believed for a moment that he would stick around. Once he knew her better, realized that she would never play his game, give in, settle for a mere physical relationship, he would move on. At least David had married her, but then even he, in short order, had walked away. Oh, he'd said that it was for her own good, that she deserved a man she could love with her whole heart, a man she could love more than her work, but what he'd really meant was that he was bored to tears being her husband.

''I don't suppose I can argue with that,'' he said.

''Then it's settled. We understand each other?''

''So long as you don't try to walk away from the team.''

Charly took a deep breath, feeling a mixture of

relief and intense disappointment, then she nodded. "All right."

The car turned into the fenced parking lot where her own small, sensible sedan waited. "I have just one favor to ask," Darren said, turning slightly toward her.

"What's that?"

He reached out for her, clasped a hand at the back of her head, near her nape. "This," he whispered, pulling her toward him.

He lowered his mouth to hers, and her eyes clamped shut. She knew she should be pushing him away, but she didn't. She couldn't. Instead she felt him slide closer and press her head back onto his shoulder. She felt his hand on her arm, turning her toward him, urging her closer. Then his arm slid around her, holding her upper body tight against his chest. His tongue nudged against her teeth, and she parted them, allowing him access. He swept the cavern of her mouth, slowly, sweetly, with aching thoroughness, as if it was the last time.

The last time.

Yes, that would be it. They could never share another kiss, another moment of this burning intimacy. Tears gathered behind her lowered lids. With poignant regret, she gave herself up to this moment, granting herself a glimpse of what might have been, of what she lost with this decision. Sliding her hands up to his shoulders and then around his neck, she yielded as completely as she dared.

His moan told her that he sensed her surrender,

welcomed it, perhaps even treasured it in some way. His mouth grew more urgent against hers, his arms tightening. Instinctively she moved her lips beneath his, rolling her head slightly side to side until it seemed that some part of him, some essence of him, seeped beneath her skin and pervaded her soul. In some indefinable way, they were joined, melded. For the last time. The only time.

Breath expended, she finally turned her head away a bit. His lips clung to hers, then broke away, returning again and again in small, nipping kisses that wound sobs tight in her chest until she could bear no more. Straightening, she pulled away, breaking contact while she still possessed the strength to do so.

"Charly," he breathed wonderingly. "Oh, Charly."

She marshaled her resources, placed before her mind's eye a picture of her son's beautiful, solemn face, and sucked in a deep breath. "I have to go. Ponce is waiting."

Darren nodded glumly. "Thank you for meeting me tonight. For letting me kiss you once more."

She cleared her throat and reached for the door handle, aware for the first time really that the limo had come to a complete halt, probably some time ago. "Goodbye, Darren."

"Goodbye."

She wanted to thank him for all he'd done for the team, but she dared not linger long enough to do so. Opening the door, she got out and walked as steadily as she could to her own automobile, firmly believing that she was walking away from what might have been one of the sweetest interludes of her life. *For Ponce,* she told herself. Only for Ponce.

Darren watched her move across the parking lot, her gait not quite as steady as she surely would have liked. Once she'd unlocked the door and gotten in behind the steering wheel of her car, he sighed and ran a hand through his hair. He hadn't counted on this. He hadn't counted on any woman, let alone this one, being able to move him as Charly did.

He sat there in the cool interior of the humming limo and faced it. This wasn't about sex, not *merely* sex, not any longer—if ever it had been. This, oddly enough, was about life, about the strange, unexpected turns it could take. He'd never expected that his life would take this particular turn. He'd never thought to find a woman, *the* woman, meant for him. He'd never expected that he actually had a mate, and yet there she was, driving away from him, sure that she had just dismissed him from her life. As if he would let her get away now!

He thought of his sister, Jill, how pleased she would be if he married, and of Ponce, who needed a father as badly as he needed a mother, of himself without them. Darren curled his hand into a fist and brought it down lightly against his knee. He supposed this was love. What else could it be? What

else could have him thinking of marriage and fa-
therhood?

And Charly expected him to just slink away, forget her and Ponce and the way she'd curled his toes
just now. Foolish woman. Sweet, foolish woman.
Shifting in his leather seat, trying to find a more
comfortable position until his need of her abated,
he began planning his next move.

Oh, he was aware that Charly thought he'd
agreed to leave her alone, but he hadn't really said
or meant that at all. She wouldn't be pleased when
she realized it, but he'd find a way to work past her
defenses. He already knew the way, in fact. Ponce.
Winning Ponce meant winning Charly. Darren was
sure of that. So, for now, he would concentrate on
the boy. It wouldn't be easy, but he would find a
way, for all their sakes, and in the end Charly would
surely love him for it.

Leaning forward, he hit the intercom button.
"Take me home, Pat."

"Yes, sir."

Smiling to himself, he wondered if Ponce would
like the penthouse or if they would all wind up
living in Charly's girlhood home. He rather fancied
that notion himself, for a while at least. Then perhaps they would build. Yes, that would be grand,
designing and building a home with Charly and
Ponce. He'd build them a mansion, a castle, some
place large enough for all their children.

That thought surprised him. All their children.
Yes, he wanted more children. How he got them

didn't matter a whit to him. Perhaps Charly couldn't have any. Perhaps that's why she and David Bellamy had never had any together, why she was so desperate to adopt Ponce. It didn't matter. Nothing would stand in the way of their happiness. He simply wouldn't allow it. He was D. K. Rudell, after all. That thought brought him up short.

Somehow he had to find a way to tell Charly. He couldn't let her go on thinking he was Darren Rudd, and yet it would take just the right words to explain it to her. Perhaps he'd best win over Ponce first, then confess all. How upset could she be? Darren Rudd was obviously no pauper, but D. K. Rudell was one of the wealthiest men in Texas. Surely that counted for something. Pushing that thought aside, he concentrated on finding a way to win Ponce's trust and affection—and the hand of the woman he loved.

Chapter Seven

The limo dropped him within feet of his private elevator. He thanked Pat, dropped a twenty through the window of the long, sleek car, although he already paid the fellow a handsome monthly salary, and strolled toward the elevator, humming even as he glanced about to be sure no one lay in wait. He safely reached the elevator, but the door did not open when it should have. Puzzled, Darren tried again. When he had no luck this time, he activated the intercom.

"Security."

"Hi." Turning, Darren waved to the tiny camera mounted high in one corner of the elevator nook. "Access pad isn't working down here. I can't get the elevator door to open."

"I'll bypass the system, Mr. Rudell, and open it

for you," came the smooth, impersonal voice from the speaker grate in the front panel of the elevator bank. "It'll take a few minutes, sir."

"No problem. But send someone down here to check this out."

"Yes, sir."

Darren slipped his hands into his pockets and rocked back on his heels, patiently waiting for the local access bypass to work. Two seconds later Tawny slunk around the corner.

"Oh, no," Darren said, yanking his hands free, "I'm not doing this." He started toward the stairway, but Tawny got to the door before him and put her back to it.

"If you know what's good for you, you'll listen to me!" she threatened in a low, feral voice.

"You have nothing to say that I want to hear," Darren told her flatly, turning toward the parking garage. Tawny zipped in front of him and lifted both arms to block his way.

"You owe me, dammit!"

Now that was too much. "Owe you?" he scoffed. "For what? Letting you live here free for more than a year?"

"I paid my rent on my back, and you know it!" she screamed.

Darren shook his head, gaping. "You value your services much too highly." With that, he punched the intercom button.

"Security."

"Never mind the bypass. I'll take the front elevator."

"It won't take long now, sir," came the puzzled reply.

"Too long, present company considered," Darren muttered and turned away, prepared to push past Tawny. To his surprise she stepped aside and folded her arms. He walked past her determinedly, but no sooner had he rounded the corner than he was snagged by the arm forcefully enough to spin him partway around.

"Oh, no, you don't," Tawny snarled, pushing her face up next to his. "I'm warning you, Darren. I've waited a long time for a setup like this, and I'm not walking away empty-handed."

Darren jerked his arm free of her grasp and stepped back. "You are some piece of work. You planned this whole thing, didn't you, from the start? You set out to seduce me, and I was all too happy to let you do it. Then you got yourself thrown out by your roommate, probably thinking I'd let you move in with me."

She didn't even try to deny it, just lifted her chin smugly. "It would have been so much simpler if you'd just taken me home with you, but no, you had to go the honorable route, setting me up in an apartment instead. Does it make you feel like some kind of god, throwing around your money and playing hard to get?"

"Impossible to get, you mean," Darren corrected. "You must have thought for sure that you could pull me back into your bed once you were living in the same building. Well, you severely overestimated your allure. Your living here just gave me the excuse I needed to move on, a very convenient excuse, I might add. Saved me the trouble of having to explain how very little you actually meant to me.''

She slapped him. Darren's head snapped to the side. He clamped his jaw, the muscles working as he ground his teeth, hands balling into fists. After a moment, however, he reined in his anger.

''All right, I deserved that, but that's the end of it, Tawny. You've got forty-eight hours,'' he said, looking her squarely in the eyes. ''If you're not gone by then, I'm calling my attorney.''

''You do that,'' Tawny sneered, ''then you get out your checkbook.''

''Why should I? I owe you nothing,'' he stated flatly.

''You can afford it.''

''And that's reason enough in your mind?'' He shook his head. ''I really thought you had more self-respect than this, Tawny.''

''You think I care about that?'' she sneered. ''All I care about is the money, so save your psychoanalysis, and get it through your head that if you want me out of your life, you're going to have pay and pay big time.''

''You were never *in* my life, Tawny.''

She folded her arms beneath her impressive bust and tossed back her mane of hair. ''Nevertheless, you'll pay,'' she said smugly. ''You could've played and paid, but, no, you're too good for that. Still, you're going to pay through the nose. I'll see to it.''

He didn't dignify the threat with a reply, just turned and walked away, preferring to hike out of the garage and around to the front of the building and the elevators in the lobby there than spend one more moment in her company. He couldn't know that once he was out of sight she would rip the front of her blouse, muss her hair, rub red spots on her neck, put on a terrified expression and stumble back into camera view, sobbing.

Darren smiled and waved as he walked onto the field. Surprised, Charly whistled the action to a stop, picked up the ball to prevent any unsupervised tussling over it, and strolled toward him. The day had turned warm, and the man wore a pair of shorts really well, darn him. Her insides tightened at the sight of those long, muscular thighs. Nevertheless, she didn't spare breath for greetings.

"What are you doing here?"

"What do you mean?" he returned innocently.

"I thought we had an understanding."

"We did. We do."

"But you said if one of us had to give up the team, it would be you."

"If," he pointed out succinctly. Then very quietly he asked, "Are you making me give up the team, Charly?"

"No, I'm not *making* you. I just thought—"

Darren's shifting gaze warned her that she was no longer able to speak freely. Smiling broadly, he went down on one knee and reached out to tousle a small head. "Hi, Ponce. How ya doin'? You were looking good out there just now. I'm proud of you. In fact, I think you're ready to start learning how to dribble the ball. What do you say to that?''

Ponce looked up at Charly, shrugged and said, ''Kay.''

''Great. Then why don't I take you and Kental down to the other end of the field to work on our dribbling skills while your mom drills the rest of the team. How would that be?'' He looked up at Charly then and said, ''I mean, if it's all right with you.''

Charly bit her lip. Obviously, while he was not ready to give up the team entirely, he was trying to stay away from her as she'd asked. She looked at Ponce, who stood staring solemnly up at her, waiting for her decision along with Darren. If she said no, who would teach Ponce and Kental to dribble, whatever that was, and how would she explain the decision? Finally she nodded at Darren. ''Sounds fine.'' She turned and waved at Kental, calling out, ''Kental, you come over here and work with Ponce and Coach Darren.''

Darren rose as the boy trotted over. Then without another word for Charly, he positioned himself between the two boys, placed a hand on each of their backs and moved them toward the opposite end of the field, saying, ''We'll need a ball. I'll demonstrate the technique, then you two can try it.''

''I'll get us a ball,'' Kental volunteered, running toward the sideline.

''We'll meet you at the other end,'' Darren called. Charly could hear him speaking to Ponce as they walked away side by side. "Now, don't worry if you don't get the technique right away. It just takes practice."

Ponce nodded, and Darren reached down quite naturally to take his small hand in his own much larger one. Charly turned away quickly, her heart in her throat.

Half an hour later they went into a fifteen-minute scrimmage, with Kental and Ponce on opposite sides so both groups had an equal chance of scoring. Kental had a strong leg and loved to boot the ball, but Ponce carefully practiced what Darren had taught him, moving the ball down the field by lightly kicking it back and forth between his feet. He concentrated so hard, looking down at his feet and the ball, that he ran into a couple of kids, but he was obviously getting the hang of it. Darren shouted encouragement from the sidelines.

"That's it, Ponce! Watch where you're going. Look at the goal. That's it! Line it up. Line it up. Shoot! Shoot!"

After carefully positioning the ball, Ponce shot it at the goal. It bounced off the upright. Kental promptly booted it into the net, completely forgetting that it wasn't his goal. Charly briefly closed her eyes. Darren covered his mouth with his hand, cleared his throat, then called out, "Okay, good work, both of you. Ponce, next time don't take the ball in quite so close. Kental remember that for today your goal and Ponce's aren't the same." He clapped his hands. "Take it in from the sideline, Sarah."

Charly had the whistle between her teeth, ready to call a halt to practice when Ponce finally managed to line up the ball again and take his shot on goal. It soared right past Tulia's head and glanced off her upraised hand, landing harmlessly outside the net. Nevertheless, Darren leaped up and punched the air, yelling, "Yes!" He glanced at Charly and exclaimed, "Dang, that kid's good!" Then, as if realizing he might be showing bias, he turned back toward the field, clapped his hands together and called out, "Great move, Tulia! Good work, everyone!"

Kental ran up and grabbed the ball, dropped it on the ground and began practicing the technique Darren had tried to teach him and Ponce. He kept kicking it too hard, but even after Charly whistled practice to an end, he continued working on the movement. Ponce began trying to demonstrate the technique for the other boy, and Darren jogged out on the field to offer some expert instruction. Charly sent off the rest of the kids with hugs and pats, then gathered up the equipment and loaded it into the trunk of her car while keeping an eye on the activity continuing on the field.

Darren used a good deal of positive reinforcement, and Kental's technique was definitely improving, as was Ponce's. Finally Kental's father honked the horn of his minivan, and Darren sent the boy off the field. He spoke a moment longer to Ponce, then gathered him in for a quick hug before jogging off toward his vehicle with a wave in

Charly's direction. Ponce watched until Darren got into his car and Charly called to him.

"Ready to go?"

Ponce parked the ball on his hip and ran toward her. "Kental likes to kick it far," he announced, "Oh, boy, he can kick it a long way more than me! But Coach Darren says you gots to play smart and dribbleding is a smart way even if I didn't score."

"Scoring doesn't count in practice, anyway," she reminded. "What counts in practice is learning, and you sure learned something new today."

"Yeah," Ponce agreed, smiling ear-to-ear. "Coach Darren says I'm the best dribbleder."

"You sure are," she told him, wishing she could hug Darren Rudd.

With the parade on Saturday morning, Charly felt it necessary to call Darren and inquire how he meant to pull the float.

"Not to worry," he said, "I've taken care of it."

"Oh. All right. I...I mean, I was sure that you would."

"But you had to check," he said. "I understand."

"Well, I guess I'll see you then."

"I'll be there," he assured her, "but I'll keep my distance."

"I'm not worried," she told him lightly.

"Good," he replied just as lightly. "Well, see ya."

"See ya."

She hung up feeling as if she'd been rushed off

the line. But then, that was what she wanted, wasn't it? Maybe *wanted* wasn't the right word, but it was necessary, expected—except that it rather unexpectedly rankled.

It rankled again when Darren showed up on Saturday morning driving a brand-new, Comet-yellow SUV with dealer tags still attached. For one insane moment she thought he might have had it specially painted to match the team colors, but then she remembered that yellow was a popular color on this particular make and model. Still, she couldn't help feeling that he had gone too far this time.

"Please tell me you didn't buy this just to pull our float!"

"Of course not," he replied, laughing. "I borrowed it from a friend."

"What friend would loan you a brand-new SUV?" she demanded skeptically.

He leaned a hip against the grill and said, "The dealer, actually. It makes for good PR, you know."

Charly felt downright stupid. "Oh."

"If I was going to buy an SUV," he told her, pushing away from the vehicle to walk around back where the trailer waited to be hooked up, "I'd buy a much larger one, something I could get at least half the team in. And I'd buy blue, not yellow."

She followed. The man was speaking to her, after all, but when he turned, grinned and parked his hands on his hips, she backed up again, shaking her head. "You didn't."

"Unfortunately I can't get the thing for nearly a

month. That particular color of blue was harder to come by than I realized.''

"Darren!'' she scolded.

"It was time to trade, anyway,'' he told her matter-of-factly. "You should've seen my bud's face when I told him I was going the SUV route, though.'' He chuckled.

She could only shake her head. "Guess you've been driving the luxury sedan for a while.''

"Actually, it was the sports car I traded. I don't think you've ever seen it. Haven't driven it much lately.''

"How many cars do you own?'' she asked.

"Uh, just three. Well, five, but my mom and sister drive a couple of them.''

Just three. Well, five. At least one of them in a team color. And at least one of them a limo. Shaking her head, she just turned and walked away. He provided cars for his mom and sister. He spent money like water and could apparently afford it. He sponsored and coached Little League soccer, spent countless hours gluing crepe paper to cardboard. He loved and praised and really taught those kids. He cooked, for pity's sake. And he curled her toes. This was the man she was doing her best to drive away. Surely she was out of her mind.

Ponce scored the winning goal in that afternoon's game. The whole team was highly pumped after the parade, and Darren drove straight to the soccer field with the float still in tow. By the time they got on the field, no team in their group could have beaten

them. It wasn't pretty. In point of fact, it was downright hilarious at times. Ponce was so intent on his
"dribbleding" that he fairly mesmerized the other
team, who at one point just stopped and stood aside
to watch him shuttle the ball down the field by
bouncing it off one foot and then the other, a mi-
crostep at a time. When he finally got it to the goal,
his shot went about three yards wide. The next one,
however, couldn't have been executed with more
precision. The other team got one shot, straight at
Tulia's chest. Both teams spent the rest of the time
bumping into one another, kicking themselves flat
onto their backs, and one little boy—thankfully on
the other team—grabbed his crotch and ran off the
field loudly proclaiming that he had to go wee-wee.

By the time it was over, Charly was as exhausted
as if she'd played every moment herself. Darren
grabbed several of the kids in a group hug and
whirled them around in celebration. Then he
hoisted Ponce onto his shoulders and proclaimed
him a "shooting star." Afterward Darren said he'd
take the trailer to the limo lot, strip it and return
the SUV to the dealer. Several of the parents offered to drop by to help him tear down the float,
and Darren gladly accepted, but when Charly said
she'd drop Ponce at her grandmother's and come
over to help, he told her that there was no need.

"We can manage," he said with a dismissive
smile. Then he turned to Ponce. "Hey, buddy, if
your mom doesn't mind, I'm thinking we might get
in a little extra practice, you and me and Kental and
Calvin. What do you think? Want to stop by your

neighborhood park for a couple hours on Sunday afternoon?''

Ponce shrugged and looked at his mother, but Charly wasn't fooled. She saw the eagerness in his eyes. Kental and Calvin, who had overheard, were already pressing their parents for permission.

"I'll pick them up if it's okay," Darren announced.

"You sure you don't mind?" Calvin's mom asked Darren.

"No, I'd like to."

"Well, all right then."

"Pick you up about one," Darren said to Kental and Calvin, "and have you home by three-thirty." He glanced up at their parents, adding, "If that's okay."

"Maybe I'll come along," Kental's dad, Lawton, suggested.

"Hey, that'd be great," Darren said heartily. "We'll make it a guy thing."

Lawton squeezed his son's shoulders. Calvin's father was deceased, and his plump, graying mother was worn out from raising three older daughters and Calvin on her own. She obviously welcomed even a single morning's respite and any male influence she could find for her son.

"We'll have to hurry home from church," Charly announced, "but Ponce will be ready." Though the expression on her son's face didn't change by so much as a flicker, she knew that he was very pleased.

"See you guys tomorrow, then," Darren said, dancing away.

Ponce slipped his hand into hers and asked softly, "What'll you do?"

Charly smiled. "Paint my toenails," she decided suddenly. "Soak in a hot tub, give myself a facial, read a good book."

He wrinkled his nose in an expression of mild distaste, then sighed as if to say she could surely come up with something more fun. Charly laughed. Ponce smiled, and she knew he was already planning his afternoon in the park with "the guys."

Money was a fine thing, but Darren quickly learned that the fun a couple guys could have with three kids, a ball of twine and a handful of dollar kite kits was priceless. Lawton brought the kites along, five of them. As he slid into the front seat of the sedan, he grinned at Darren and said, "For after that special practice."

"Aw, we can practice soccer anytime," Darren replied flippantly.

Lawton chuckled. "I didn't think you were serious about that."

Kental had definitely inherited his tall, athletic build from his father, but not his ebullient, chatty personality. Lawton was a quiet, deep man who seemed comfortable with himself and everyone around him. Darren liked him immensely but had been surprised when he'd invited himself along on this outing.

The park was crowded, the weather being fine if

a bit chilly, and the boys joined the throng on the playground while Lawton and Darren snapped together the kites. "The slats were made of wood when I was a boy," Lawton commented idly, holding up a thin, square, plastic tube.

"My sister and I made sails out of painted newspaper," Darren said, pulling the plastic sheeting into place over the plastic frame.

"You weren't always rich, then," Lawton said evenly.

"Nope."

Lawton tied on a plastic tail and asked bluntly, "So how'd you do it? I mean, you're not smug about it, but it's obvious you're the man with the money."

Darren sent him a level look. "Want the truth?" Lawton nodded. "Luck. Pure luck. Right place, right product field, right time."

"Maybe luck started it," Lawton said doubtfully, "but you must've made the right decisions and worked real hard to get where you are."

"Yeah, I have," Darren admitted unabashedly.

"Me," Lawton said with a sigh, "I made all the wrong decisions. Dropped out of high school to get married when Shemetra got pregnant with our oldest girl. Not that I don't love my wife and kids, you understand, but the only way to make money in construction, which is all I know, is to own the business, and that takes money."

"Maybe you should consider a start-up loan."

Lawton snorted. "Yeah, right. What bank is gonna take a chance on me? I don't even own the house I live in, got no credit—though no debt, either, I'm glad to say—and Yolanda is talking about college.'' He shook his head regretfully. "She's smart as a whip, that girl, tenth in her class, but tenth doesn't translate into much scholarship money.''

Darren studied Lawton intently. Everything he knew about the man told him that Lawton was a caring, concerned father doing the best he could in his circumstances, and Darren knew that he had the power to change those circumstances. "Tell you what you do,'' Darren said carefully, "you put together a plan, what kind of jobs you expect to find and where you'll find them, how many employees you'll need, what equipment, how much money it will take to get through the first six months or so, and if it's reasonable, workable, I'll back you for a percentage of the profits.''

Lawton sat there for several seconds just staring at him, but Darren could see the wheels spinning behind his dark eyes, the plans forming. Finally Lawton grinned. "Looks like my lucky day finally came.''

Darren smiled, and they each went back to kite building.

By the end of the afternoon, Darren felt happy and relaxed. Calvin had lost two kites, even though the second had been tied to his wrist. The boys had giggled and tussled and generally run themselves ragged. Their clothing was stained with powdered sugar and brightly colored syrup from the funnel cakes and drinks with which they'd stuffed themselves. Ponce had stood on Darren's shoulders to extract his own errant kite from the clutches of a tree and accepted a boost at a water fountain. Later, too exhausted to move, he'd leaned against Darren as they sat on a bench gathering their strength, then he'd allowed Darren to pull him onto his lap to make room for Calvin.

On the way home, Darren dropped off Calvin first. Before leaving Lawton and Kental in front of their rented house not far from the practice field, he made an appointment with Lawton on an evening at the end of the coming week. He drove Ponce across town in silence, thinking that the boy had fallen asleep in the back seat. He was very surprised, then, when Ponce suddenly said, "You don't have to take me places just 'cause you like my mom."

Darren glanced into the rearview mirror, saw nothing and pulled over to the side of the street. Sliding the transmission into park, he turned in his seat to look over his shoulder at Ponce. "You seem to be saying that you think I don't like you."

Ponce looked away. "You like my mom," he repeated accusingly.

"I'm wild about your mom," Darren admitted bluntly. "But what makes you think I don't like you?"

Ponce shrugged. "You wouldn't take me to the park if you didn't like my mom."

"I wouldn't have even met you if I didn't like your mom," Darren pointed out. "I got involved in this whole soccer thing just so I could get to know your mom, and because of that I met you and Calvin and Lawton and Kental and all the rest of the kids. And now I have a lot of new friends, and I like your mom even more than I did before. So now tell me why you think I don't like you.''

'''Cause I'm in the way!'' Ponce yelled. ''I'm always in the way!''

''If you think that,'' Darren told him evenly, managing to keep his voice level despite the emotion wringing his heart, ''you don't really know anything about Charly or me. She loves you. She wants you. She's doing her best to adopt you so you'll always be part of her life. And because I care so much for her, I want that, too. You're not in anyone's way, Ponce. You *are* the way. You are the way to happiness for Charly and me.''

Ponce considered that, his round eyes growing so large that they seemed to engulf his whole face. ''That don't mean you got to take me places,'' he finally mumbled.

''Well, it means I have to do something,'' Darren said, letting the boy see his frustration and need. ''I want Charly. You're part of her. She needs you, and you need her. She won't see me, even though she does like me, because it makes *you* uncomfortable. All I know to do, Ponce, is to help you get to know me, so you're not afraid I'll take your mom away from you and do bad things to you. If you can trust me, if you can like me as much as I like you, we can all be happy. But without you, nobody around here gets to be really happy.''

The boy's high brow wrinkled. He turned his

head, obviously thinking about all Darren had said. Suddenly his head snapped around and he said, "You got a lotta money, don't you?"

"Yes, I do," Darren admitted flatly. "And you know something, it's good, having money. You can do a lot of good things with money, and you can have a lot of fun, but money by itself isn't enough, Ponce. When you have a lot of money, people treat you differently. They want to be your friends for the wrong reasons, not because they know you or like you. That's when money gets in the way, because you need someone to share it with, to use it for, or it's meaningless. I'm hoping that you and Charly will let me share myself with you. I need you to give me a chance, Ponce."

The boy just stared at him. After a moment, Darren turned around and drove Ponce home.

He walked Ponce to the door, uncertain whether he'd made headway or not. Charly greeted them with nervous smiles. Suddenly animated, Ponce threw himself into his mother's waiting arms. "We flew kites! And had funny cakes and cherry coolers, and I stood up in a tree on top of Darren."

Charly's brows rose at that. "What he means," Darren explained, "is that he stood on my shoulders to get his kite out of a tree."

"Yeah," Ponce agreed, nodding. "It was fun! But Calvin let go two kites that went way, way up till you couldn't even see 'em no more. Kental's dad said they got lost in the sun."

Darren smiled at that. Merriment twinkled in Charly's eyes. "What about practice?"

Darren cleared his throat. "Uh, we didn't exactly get to that."

"I see."

"It was all Lawton's fault," Darren said, chuckling. "He brought the kites."

She laughed. "Well, boys will be boys, I guess."

"I won't even bother to deny it," he said with mock solemnity. She laughed again, and he couldn't help grinning, pleased with himself. The moment would never be better. *Here goes,* he thought, marveling at how nervous he felt, and plunged in. "I'm not boy enough to go alone to an animated movie, though, so maybe you guys will go with me? I want to see the movie, so I really need Ponce as an excuse."

To his surprise and satisfaction, Ponce begged to go. "Can we, Mom? Can we? Please?"

Charly split a look between Darren and her son. "Oh, uh, I don't think you need me. You two go."

"No, you come, too, Mama," Ponce pleaded. "Please. It'll be fun!"

Darren sent the boy a grateful look, which was studiously ignored, before saying gently to Charly, "Please."

She seemed confused, suspicious, and he was certain that she was going to refuse, but then she nodded. Relief coursed through him, making him almost giddy. He wanted desperately to reach for her, to pull her against him. Instead, he turned Ponce to him, crouched and told that boy with his eyes how grateful he was, before ruffling his hair and looping his arms about him in a loose hug.

Some of the old wariness slipped back in as Ponce stiffened slightly. Darren released him immediately and rose to his full height. With a wave and a smile, he left them there, absolutely delighted to be looking forward to an animated movie with a five-year-old and his mother. What would the society and gossip columns make of that? He could almost see the headline.

Playboy Playing Dad at Local Movie Theater.

Darren was beginning to think that it was a role at which he could excel, given half a chance. It was a chance he found that he wanted very much.

Charly couldn't imagine why she'd done it. Just days ago she'd told him to back off, and today she'd agreed to a movie date with him and her son. What was it about Darren Rudd that she just couldn't seem to resist? And what had happened to change Ponce's attitude? She should be wary, and she was. Still, excitement coursed through her veins because suddenly she felt…hope.

Oh, this was foolish in the extreme. She was just looking for a broken heart, and yet she was going to that movie. She and her son were going to that movie with Darren Rudd. God help her.

Chapter Eight

They went to the movies, not just the one movie but every kid movie out there. They ate dinner in fast-food restaurants, eating amidst the chaos of playgrounds teeming with screaming children. The food was horrendous. Darren enjoyed every moment of it. He felt, oddly, as if he was really living for the first time, living not playing, and he believed he was making progress toward his goal.

As Ponce grew more comfortable with him, Charly seemed more at ease, more accepting. They shared private, adult smiles over Ponce's childish antics, tastes and manner of speaking. She didn't move away when Darren casually slipped his arm about her shoulders during the movie. Once or twice she took his arm as they walked.

They talked, they laughed, all three of them.

Ponce fell once and hit his head. Darren was the first to reach him, and Ponce let him soothe the hurt before putting on a brave face for Charly, who just stood there, smiling and letting Darren take care of it. Darren came to believe that the boy would do anything for Charly, even accept him. That alone made Darren extremely fond of Ponce.

For Charly he felt great respect, a surprising affinity and shocking lust, even by his standards. The sight of a loose bra strap that kept slipping from beneath the sleeveless shoulder of her blouse had him painfully aroused for an entire evening. A bra strap! A very sensible, unadorned—not even a scrap of lace!—bra strap. The curve of her neck intrigued him for hours. He couldn't keep his hands out of her hair. Her mouth mesmerized him. When she spoke, he'd get lost in the shape and movement of those rosy lips, the curl of that pink tongue, the straight, even edges of her white teeth. She was the smartest, sexiest, most endearing and utterly innocent creature he'd every met. He supposed that altogether it could comprise nothing less than love, and he had to bite his tongue from time to time to keep from blurting words she wouldn't want to hear. Yet.

He believed in *yet*. He had no choice. For to believe that she would not eventually come to care for him was impossible, unbearable. He forgot that she didn't know his real name. It hardly seemed to matter, since she knew the real him, the person he was inside and had only a nodding acquaintance with himself. She knew he was wealthy, and more

than the minor executive he had seemed in the beginning. What difference did a last name make?
What did it matter who he had been before, how
he had played at living? All that mattered was
Charly and Ponce, nothing else.

Darren was so wrapped up in the two of them
that when he realized Tawny had not moved out
within the time limit, he merely sighed and made a
mental note to call his personal lawyer, but he
couldn't seem to be outraged or troubled. Tawny
was the past. Charly and Ponce were the future. He
couldn't see anyone else or any outcome but the
one he so wanted. All his creative energy, all his
deepest thoughts, all his dearest plans were an-
chored in the two of them. Tawny was so far from
his mind that he didn't even bother to avoid her,
and since she didn't put herself in his way, he had
no reason to spare her any but the most cursory
thought.

He was much too happy, much too hopeful to
worry about anything more than whether or not
Charly would keep him at arm's length until after
the adoption was finalized, and his own patience
both surprised and entertained him. The playboy
had been domesticated by a bleeding-heart attorney
with a loose bra strap and a too-wise adoptive son.
Life was just damned good.

She was playing with fire, and she knew it, but
no matter how Charly scolded herself in private,
when Darren showed up, when he called, when he
smiled down at Ponce and rubbed his hand over the

boy's head, all her resolve evaporated. It was so easy to be with Darren, even for Ponce. She asked him one evening if he liked Darren now, and he glanced at her, shrugged and said, "Yeah, sure. He's a good guy."

"It doesn't bother you that he comes around all the time?"

Ponce shook his head. His eyes narrowed slightly, and he grinned, waggling a finger at her. "You like him."

"Does *that* bother you?"

He bit his lip and admitted, "A little bit. But it's all right 'cause I'm not in the way."

"Of course you're not in the way! You could never be in the way."

"I know."

"I love you."

"I know." She put her arms around him. He snuggled into the crook of her arm and looked up at her. "You need me," he said matter-of-factly.

She tapped the end of his nose. "That's right. How did you know?"

"Darren told me."

Her heart stopped. "Darren?"

Ponce nodded nonchalantly and turned back to the television program he had been watching. She didn't have to think very long to realize that Darren had made Ponce see that he would not be shunted aside, that he was accepted, an integral part of all that went on around her. Maybe the future held more than wishful thinking for them, after all.

Maybe they had more to look forward to than soccer and movies and hamburgers.

She agreed to go out with him, real dates, just
the two of them. They interspersed those evenings
with time spent with Ponce, and Charly had to admit, albeit privately, that Darren Rudd fitted perfectly into the scheme of their lives, especially her
own.

One evening when she'd made a date to go out
to dinner and a play with Darren, Ponce wanted to
spend the night with Kental, but Charly felt better
knowing that he and Kental would be at her house
with her grandmother. Besides, it would give Darren a chance to actually meet Delphina—and Delphina a chance to meet Darren.

He arrived with flowers, dressed in a pair of fluid,
dark-gray slacks and a light-gray silk sweater with
short sleeves and a banded neck. Charly had chosen
a simple sleeveless sheath in bright orange and a
short, soft, dark-red cardigan sweater with long
sleeves and a single pearl button closure. The heat
in his gaze told her that she looked good.

"Granna, this is Darren Rudd. Darren, my grandmother, Delphina Michman."

"It's a pleasure to meet you, ma'am. I've heard
so much about you."

"Oh, and I've heard so much about you," Delphina returned, glancing meaningfully at Ponce.

Darren grinned and waggled his eyebrows.
"Yeah? Maybe we should compare notes sometime."

Delphina chuckled. "Sometime."

Charly sent her grandmother a warning glare and excused herself to hurry into the kitchen to hunt up a vase large enough to accommodate the big bouquet of tulips he'd brought. When she returned after several minutes of frantic searching with the tulips hastily arranged in a chipped vase, she found Darren crouched down with Ponce on the floor, carefully bending the axle of a tiny car so that the front wheels would turn freely.

"That'll work as long as you don't crash it," he said, giving the car a shove with his index finger.

"Thanks," Ponce said, and to Charly's shock, the boy bounced up and kissed Darren on the cheek. Darren ruffled Ponce's curly hair and smiled. Only then did he see her standing there. His smile broadened as he rose to his full height.

"All set? Pat's waiting out front with the engine running."

"You didn't bring the limo!"

Darren winked at Delphina and said, "Hey, I cracked a bottle of champagne earlier. You wouldn't want me to drink and drive, would you?"

"You like being ostentatious," Charly accused without the least heat.

He didn't deny it. She placed the tulips on the mantel and gave them a final tweak. Delphina chuckled. Charly hugged Ponce and kissed him, told him to be a good boy and not to play too roughly with Kental. She instructed Delphina to apologize for her for not waiting to greet Kental's parents when they dropped him off, then finally allowed an impatient Darren to usher her out of the house.

"Where are we going for dinner?" she asked as he handed her down into the car.

"That depends on you," he told her, sliding in beside her. "My personal preference would be my place. I make a mean stir fry."

Her pulse sped up and not because of the stir fry. It was a pity she had to decline. "I don't think that's a good idea."

Nodding resignedly, he sat forward to instruct the driver to take them to a Chinese restaurant in Addison. "You do like Chinese, don't you?"

"Love it."

"Then you ought to like this place."

She looked at him suspiciously. "Don't tell me you own it."

He laughed and said, "I've never even been there, but it comes highly recommended."

"Oh."

The conversation didn't lag. He immediately said, "Your grandmother is one sharp old tack."

"The sharpest."

"As soon as you left the room, she said to me, 'So you're the rich dog whose been sniffing around my granddaughter.'"

Charly gasped, her face flaming. "She didn't!"

"You know she did," he replied, grinning.

Charly groaned and asked warily, "What did you say?"

"I said that I'd be doing more than sniffing if I could get away with it."

"Darren!"

"Hey, I believe in the value of the truth."

Charly's face burned hotly. "Did Ponce hear any of this?"

"Yeah. He laughed. That boy knows a lot more than he should, and yet he's somehow untouched by it."

"You're right," she said pensively. "You're absolutely right."

"Can I kiss you now or are you going to make me wait?" he asked suddenly, sliding his arm about her shoulders.

"Has anyone ever made you wait for anything?" she asked wryly.

"Only you," he said, leaning his forehead against hers, "but for you I'll wait as long as it takes."

Heart pounding, she slipped her arms around his neck. "Just a kiss," she warned.

"Just a kiss," he promised.

That man could make a kiss a full-body experience. The sensations were so extreme that they were almost painful. By the time the car pulled up in front of the restaurant, need throbbed embarrassingly in the most sensitive and private parts of her body.

Darren sat back and rubbed a hand over his face, huffing great breaths of air. He swallowed, slid an incredulous look in her direction and asked pointedly, "You're sure you don't want me to cook for you?"

She laid a hand over her pounding heart and got

enough breath in her lungs to say, "I'm sure I'd never get dinner if I set foot in a place any more private than this with you."

Grinning, he reached for her again, pulling her close. "You are absolutely right, but then you usually are. I want you so badly it hurts, but it isn't just physical, you know. I want *you*. All of you."

She melted inside. "Darren. Thank you. That's... that's so incredible. But..."

"Ponce, I know. He's a great kid, and you're a wonderful mother, but he needs, deserves, a dad, too."

She pulled away from him in shock. "Darren?"

"Single mothers raise great kids all the time, and you're one of the best. I know that. But wouldn't it be easier, better, for everyone, if he could have two parents, if you had a husband, a partner?"

She had to close her mouth before she could stammer, "Darren, a-are you asking me t-to..."

He cupped her chin in the curve of his fingers. "All I'm asking you to do right now is think about it. I have been. A lot."

She was speechless, thrilled, a little frightened. Thrilled was dominant. Instinctively she lifted her mouth to his. His arms clasped her tight, his tongue sweeping into her mouth possessively. A car door slammed somewhere nearby, and Darren groaned, pulling back incrementally.

"In another minute even this may be too private," he muttered against her cheek. His hand fumbled behind him for the door handle, found it and yanked. The door swung open. "Come on," he growled, sliding away from her, his hand clasping hers.

Charly bit her lip as she slipped out of the car and into the crook of his arm. By the time they reached the restaurant, an odd, almost hysterical happiness had gripped her. She was still too stunned to really do as he'd asked and think about the possibility of...partnership? The word *marriage* hovered just out of reach on the periphery of her mind, and she dared not beckon it closer. Yet.

It was enough for the moment to feel his arm curled protectively about her waist, his hand resting lightly against the curve of her hip, scalding her with its possessive heat. It was enough to see the desire in his eyes, the hope. It was almost too much, this reveling in, this contemplating of love.

Love with Darren Rudd.

Sitting around with a stupid grin on his face was getting very damned little work done, and Darren couldn't even seem to care. Marketing called to report that California sales figures had fallen two full percentage points, and Darren chuckled. The director on the other end of the line was so shocked that he didn't speak for at least twenty seconds. Darren cleared his throat and said quite authoritatively that a dramatic rise in sales in Arizona, Texas and the Carolinas would more than make up for any declines. He could still feel the poor bean counter's shock when he hung up a few moments later, but how could he be concerned about a minuscule drop in sales in a single state when he was in love, planning to be married and about to become a father?

Oh, she hadn't said yes. In point of fact, he hadn't asked yet. But he'd shown his hand, and she hadn't folded hers and walked away from the table. What she had done was turn him inside out. His blood still sizzled with the heat of their good-night kisses, and though he'd spent the remainder of the night pondering how to get her to the altar quickest, he felt positively bubbling today. Very soon now he was going to sit her down and clear up this identity thing, but first maybe he ought to go shopping for a diamond ring.

He was weighing the obvious merits of confessing his little deception with a diamond in his palm when his secretary buzzed. He lifted the receiver and heard, without any preamble, "Can you see Mr. Anselm? He says it's urgent."

A mild wave of surprise rolled through him. "Walt's here?"

"He's on his way in, Mr. Rudell. I'm sorry."

Before he could tell her not to worry about it, the door to his office opened and Walter Anselm strode through it. Darren hung up the telephone receiver and sat back in his high, leather chair, surprise swelling into disquiet. "Walt, what's going on?"

A tall, slender, athletic man with thick, prematurely graying hair, a killer golf swing and buckets of oozing charm, Anselm's usual sang-froid seemed to have deserted him at the moment. His hands brushed back the sides of his charcoal-gray suit coat and landed at his waist.

"What have I told you?" he barked. "How many times have I warned you that your tomcatting was going to cost you one day?"

Darren relaxed and smiled. "Well, you'll be happy to know you can stow that particular lecture for good, my friend."

"Stow it?" Walt erupted. Reaching into his coat pocket, he extracted a sheaf of folded papers and slapped them onto Darren's desk. "I don't think so."

Darren frowned at the blue-backed papers. "What's this?"

"This," Walt said, pointing an accusing finger at the papers, "is fifteen million dollars."

"What?"

"In the form of a palimony suit," the attorney enunciated precisely, "or what passes for it in Texas."

"Palimony! That's nuts!"

"Filed by one Ms. Tawny Beekman," Walt said, forging on doggedly. Leaning forward, he planted both palms against the edge of the desk and finished with, "of *your* address."

The word that Darren blurted out then put as grim an expression on Walt Anselm's narrow face as if he actually smelled the matter called to mind. "Fifteen million dollars worth of it," the attorney confirmed flatly.

Darren shook his head in disgust, wondering how catastrophic it might be if Charly and Ponce were to learn about Tawny Beekman. Why now? Why did this have to happen now? Tawny couldn't have timed it worse. "Damn her! I do not need this!"

"What you need, randy buddy of mine," Walt pointed out, tapping an index finger against the polished desktop, "are the top guns in this particularly nasty field of litigation. Unless you're willing to settle, that is."

Darren squirmed in frustration. If he settled, it would be as good as an admission of guilt. If he didn't and lost, he would come off even worse, a complete cad and selfish into the bargain. He only had one option, to fight and win. Everything he knew about Charly told him that she would need that much corroboration. "It's bunk, Walt," he told his friend and trusted advisor. "I can't settle, and not just because I'd prefer to send myself into the poor house fighting it before I'd willingly give that conniving she-wolf a cent."

"I was afraid you'd say that," Walt muttered, scraping a hand through his hair. "That's why I called my friend Alvin Dennis of Bellows, Cartere, Dennis and Pratt. He's pulling together a team of lawyers to help us fight this, preferably one with a woman on it. Believe me, it looks a lot better to a jury and judge if it's a woman asking the tough, personal questions of the plaintiff that this kind of litigation always requires."

Darren had made the complete transition from shock to pure anger now. "Whatever, whoever it takes," he stated emphatically, even knowing that he'd have to tell Charly. Eventually. First things first, however. Once he got the ball rolling on his defense, he'd sit Charly down and tell her in unequivocal terms about his feelings and intentions toward her. Then he'd confess the truth about himself and his identity. After that he'd propose, and finally he'd tell her about Tawny and this absurd lawsuit. It seemed like a good plan.

He couldn't have conceived how it was all set to blow up in his face.

Charly, or Charlene as she was known around the office, made a face. "Richard," she said, as unemotionally as her repugnance would allow, "you know how I hate these sleazy sexual harassment cases."

"It's not a sex har," Richard Pratt, her least favorite of the partners and immediate supervisor, said. "It's a palimony."

Charly barely refrained from rolling her eyes. "Well, forgive me if it's not politically correct, but I don't have much compassion for kept women."

"We're not defending *her*," he snapped. "We're defending *him*."

"Oh, swell, let's defend the user."

Pratt parked himself on the corner of Charly's desk and regarded her owlishly over the rims of his reading glasses. "Look, Charlene, Dennis himself assigned you to the team. I don't give a rat's small behind where your compassion falls on this, you'll take the cross or you'll polish your résumé. Those are your options."

Dennis was the most senior partner. Shaken,

Charly sat back. They weren't giving her any choice, and they expected her to grill the female plaintiff! The client must be somebody important. "Somebody with deep pockets," she mumbled.

"Very deep," Richard Pratt confirmed. "The obvious plus for you is that it wipes out the deficit you've dealt this firm with your excessive pro bono work. With this one, you could turn up our top earner for the year."

Charly gritted her teeth at the term *excessive,* but she managed to keep her tone civil. "So I help some mega-rich sugar daddy walk away from the woman he's used and suddenly I'm the firm's fair-haired girl."

Pratt smiled smugly. "Shouldn't be too difficult. The 'poor used' woman is an exotic dancer. Stripper, if you want to be blunt about it."

"So naturally she's incapable of being misused and foolish enough to give us all the ammunition we need to savage her after the fact," Charly said, not bothering to rein in her sarcasm.

Pratt shifted off the desk and rose to his feet. "It must be genetic with you Bellamys," he said condescendingly. "You just naturally try to sniff out the underdogs and line up with them. Well, once you speak to our boy, I think you'll find that this case isn't quite what you expect. Even if he's not telling us the whole truth—and who does?—this is little more than an extortion attempt on her part."

Charly sighed. That would be the company line, of course, but what difference did it make? Why was she even fighting it? Steeling herself against the inevitable, she asked, "So who is our client?"

Pratt smiled smugly, never having doubted her capitulation, as if he'd given her the option. "None other than D. K. Rudell, mastermind behind RuCom Electronics."

Charly's eyebrows rose. "Interesting," she muttered.

"I should say so. He's known as one of the great playboys of our age. The gossip columns are always speculating about who he's sleeping with now. Come to think of it, I don't recall seeing anything about him recently. Must have a new playmate stashed away someplace private."

"That's *not* what I meant," Charly told him ruefully. "It's just that I happen to know someone who works for RuCom, two someones actually." She bit her lip, pondering, and finally added carefully, "One of them has to know him personally."

"Small world," Pratt commented. "Who are they? We may need to gather some background."

Charly shrugged. "My ex-husband for one. He can't tell you anything. He's pretty far down the corporate ladder, a retail manager. The other, though..." She hesitated before admitting, "I'm not even sure of his job title, but judging from his income, I'd say he's well *up* that ladder."

Sensing a juicy bit of gossip here, Pratt leaned across the desk. "And who would *he* be, hmm, this top-runger?"

Charly sat far back in her chair, as far from Richard Pratt as she could get. "Just someone I'm...a friend, just a friend."

Speculation danced in Pratt's avid little eyes. Though a tall, broad, good-looking man, some innate ingredient in Richard Pratt's makeup permanently fixed him in the category of "small." He was a fine attorney and evidently well respected if not well liked. Perhaps it was the *something* distasteful that lurked about his eyes, a hint of corruption.

"So the ice princess has a sex life, after all," he purred.

Disgust slammed through Charly. "She has a friend," Charly snapped, "a fine *gentleman* friend."

Pratt laughed. "A heterosexual gentleman, one presumes," he quipped, turning toward the door. He opened it and paused, looking over his shoulder at her. "That means he says please as he's putting it to you and thank you as he's walking away after."

"You really are a skunk," Charly said evenly.

"Client meeting tomorrow at eleven," Pratt told her, pointing to the desk and the stack of briefs and law books he'd carried into her office earlier—a starting point, as he'd called it. "I suggest you bone up."

Charly snatched up a sheet of notepaper, wadded it and threw it as hard as she could at the closing door, imagining that it was a rock bouncing off Richard Pratt's broad back. He thought he knew so much, thought all the world was as smarmy and unprincipled as he was, but he didn't know her, and he didn't know Darren Rudd.

Pratt couldn't begin to fathom a man like Darren. Richard believed that she was a freak of nature, a goody-two-shoes ruled by female emotion rather than reasoned compassion. He could never understand how a handsome, successful, sexy man like Darren could also be good and caring and generous. Pratt could never even imagine the basic decency that was such a part of Darren. It was so foreign to him that he wouldn't see it even if she rubbed his nose in it. He lacked the capacity to understand what Charly knew instinctively. Darren cared for others because he was compelled to do so, and in her heart she knew that she had found her soul mate in him. Even Ponce realized that he was no threat, liked him, even.

She would do what she had to for their client, give him the best defense that she possibly could, but as far as she was concerned, no matter how uncharitable it might be, the Richard Pratts and D. K. Rudells of this world could just go hang.

Chapter Nine

She was late. Charly slung her handbag onto her desk, grabbed a heavy book, shouldered her bulging briefcase by the strap and swung out of her office again in a heartbeat. She passed the secretarial pool in the center of the spacious reception area at a jarring clip, slowing only slightly as her friend and favorite assistant, Helen, rose from her desk.

"Have you seen this morning's papers?"

Charly shook her head as she hurried toward the conference room. "No time. Overslept. Stayed up all night reading case law."

"You'll want to take a look," Helen warned her, falling in behind with a steno pad and pen.

Charly nodded, dismissing the thought almost instantly, and shoved through the heavy door. Shoulders squared, she put on her best no-nonsense smile.

Three of the four partners were already present,
Bellows, Dennis and Pratt, arranged on two sides
of the rectangular table. She nodded apologetically
to each as she dumped her burden in front of a free
chair. "Sorry. Busy night, but I think I've got the
bases covered." She turned to Helen. "I need everything you can find on Hartley versus Brite and
Texas common law marriage."

"Common law marriage!" someone echoed.

Charly lifted a stalling hand, prepared to explain
the strategy she'd developed, even as something
struck her as familiar about that exclamation and
the voice that had made it.

"Put Newkirk and Li on it," she instructed
Helen. "Tell them to leave no stone unturned."
Nodding, Helen hurried out of the room. Charly
braced her hands against the tabletop and took a
deep breath, prepared to meet the client now, only
to realize that he was not within sight. Sensing a
presence at the window, she straightened and
turned, one hand automatically tugging at the bottom of her suit coat.

"Charly?" he said, standing in front of the large,
plate-glass window that looked down on Commerce
Street. She blinked and smiled.

"Darren! What are you doing here?"

He stared at her, solemn as a judge in a hand-
made designer suit. Slowly the hair rose on the back
of her neck, but she couldn't quite think why. She
had meant to question him in this case. Eventually.
In private. She frowned. How had Pratt known the

identity of the "friend" she'd mentioned yesterday, and why had he called Darren in for this meeting?

"I...I tried to tell you last n-night," he stammered.

She put a hand to her head, trying to make sense of what her instincts were telling her. "I know. I'm sorry. I was just so busy. I never dreamed you'd been contacted about this, but you could have mentioned it on the phone."

Suddenly the door swung open and Cartere, always the voice of doom, pushed his big belly into the room, his bald head following. "Well, it's hit the fan," he growled, slapping a heap of newspapers onto the table. "And she throws hard ball, this Tawny person."

Darren closed his eyes. Charly glanced at the newspapers. Faceup, the front page headline screamed, Stripper Sues RuCom Founder! Below it, a full spread above the fold, was a large photograph. Her attention caught, Charly tilted her head to get the best view. It was a waist-up photo of Darren in a tuxedo. The woman just behind him and obviously on his arm was a beautiful, sexy blonde with a big smile and enormous breasts, most of which were revealed by the cut of her dress.

A strange buzzing filled Charly's ears. Somewhere in the distance she heard a familiar voice saying, "I didn't realize you two already know each other."

Someone else said, "Whoever's advising Ms. Beekman is trying to force you to settle, D.K., by making their case to the press."

"Prejudicing the trial," agreed another.

Charly couldn't seem to get air into her lungs, but no matter how hard she tried, she couldn't deny the truth slapping her in the face. Darren Rudd, her Darren, her soul mate, was D. K. Rudell. She turned wide, confused eyes on him. *I believe in the value of the truth.* But even that was a lie! It was all lies, everything he'd said and done.

"Just let me explain," he pleaded, coming toward her with outstretched hands. "I wanted to tell you last night. I...I didn't know, I'm not sure I ever even asked, who you work for!"

She couldn't feel, couldn't think beyond the awful realization of her own stupidity. Why hadn't she known? Why hadn't she realized? "No," she said. "No."

"Charly, listen, when I told you my name was Rudd, I...I only wanted you to get to know the real me without the reputation and the rest of it getting in the way."

The real him. The real Darren, D. K. Rudell. She shook her head. "Oh, my God."

"Charly, sweetheart, you have to understand."

"Oh. My. God."

"I was going to tell you. If you hadn't been busy last night, I'd—"

"How could you?"

He bowed his head, and the full force of the lie buffeted her. He didn't care. He had never cared, not about her, not about Ponce, not about the team. What was a little money to him, a lot of money, even? He was D. K. Rudell, retail genius, electronics mogul. Playboy. It was all just an elaborate game, a challenge. Could Darren Rudd get the girl as easily as D. K. Rudell? Could he make the committed mother and bleeding-heart attorney fall in love with him? That he could, that he had, was like a knife to the chest. Numbly she turned and walked out of the room away from the lie, not caring if she walked away from her job, her career, as well.

He caught her in front of the secretarial pool, his strong hands turning her sharply. "Sweetheart, you have to listen to me."

The anger she hadn't quite acknowledged erupted. "Get your hands off me!" She yanked free, arms wrapping about her upper arms protectively. "Don't ever touch me again."

His hands hovered about her but didn't touch. "Honey, I'm sorry. I should've told you. I was going to."

"Spare me." Turning on her heel, she strode toward her office, mind churning. Her job. Suddenly she understood that she was going to lose her job when she needed it most, just before the hearing. Ponce! Oh, God, how could she tell him? What could she tell him? Desperation clawed at her, ripping wounds in her psyche that flowed freely, bleeding anger, shame, regret and such disappointment that it nearly felled her.

Somehow she was standing in front of her desk, but she couldn't quite think why. Then she spied her handbag. Her car keys were in that bag. She snatched it up just as Darren, D.K., whoever he was, shoved through the door.

"Charly, I love you," he said.

Laughter spilled out of her, or was it crying? "Right." She whirled on him. "And you never heard of Tawny Beekman."

He gulped. The door bumped him, shoving him forward a few stumbling steps as Richard Pratt plowed into the room. He glanced at Darren but focused a glare on Charly. "What the hell is going on?"

"I'm leaving," she said, proud that her voice shook only slightly. "Get someone else to front the case."

"Maybe I didn't make myself clear before. Your job depends—"

"Her job is *not* at risk here," Darren interrupted firmly. Pratt glanced at him in surprise. "Whether she stays or she goes, her job is not at risk," he stated bluntly. "Fire her and I'll find some other firm to represent me."

Pratt narrowed his eyes and stepped closer to Charly, hissing, "You are going to blow this for the firm."

"Shut up, Pratt," Darren ordered. Pratt snapped his mouth shut like a guppy trapping a hatchling. Darren eased in front of him. "Charly, I don't expect you to work on this case. I didn't realize you were even employed with this firm."

"Obviously," she snapped, daring him to deny that he hadn't wanted her to know about Tawny Beekman.

"Maybe you told me who you work for," he

went on, "but if you did, I don't remember. I was too busy falling in love with you."

"In love!" Pratt parroted.

"Are you still here?" Darren growled, twisting such a glare over one shoulder that the other man stumbled backward.

"B-but Mr. Rudell," he stammered. "You d-don't understand. That's Charlene Bellamy."

"I know who she is, you idiot."

"Which is more than I can say about you, or could," she pointed out sharply. "Then again, I don't make a habit of lying about my identity."

"Neither do I," Darren insisted.

"Except to me, apparently."

Darren ran a hand through his hair. "Would you have given me so much as the time of day if you'd known?"

"No more than I intend to now," she retorted, turning toward the door.

He caught her by the arm, then released her immediately, saying, "I understand why you're angry, and I don't expect you to represent me in this case, but Charly, please let me explain."

"You, your case and your explanations can go straight to hell, Mr. *Rudell*," she told him flatly. He clamped his jaw and looked away, a muscle flexing in the hollow of his cheek. It was Richard Pratt who threw himself in front of the door.

"You can't walk out!" he exclaimed. To Darren he said, "You don't understand. We need a female at the table on this, and she's the only female on staff!"

"The *only* female?" Darren repeated skeptically.

"The only attorney," Richard corrected.

"Hire another," Darren ordered.

"He can't," Charly told him smugly, folding her arms. "No self-respecting female attorney in the state will work for this firm. Their bias against women is legendary, though to give him his due, Cartere is trying to change it, without much success, sadly. I wouldn't be here if the Texas Women's Law Association hadn't filed a class-action suit against them. They were desperate for a token female by the time they got to me, and I was frankly too desperate myself to turn them down when they made me the offer."

"If you'd bring in some money," Richard snapped. He addressed Darren again. "She's an excellent attorney, but every firm in town knows she's got something against clients who can pay. Every penniless, hopeless cause in the state beats a path to her desk!"

"The law is about more than money!" Charly protested hotly.

"Can we just stick to the point?" Darren intervened. "I thought you guys were experts at my sort of case," he said to Richard Pratt.

"They are," Charly said, "but they're usually sitting on the opposite side of the courtroom."

Pratt ignored her, focusing on Darren instead. "As much as I hate to admit it," he said, drawing himself up tight, "we need her."

"*I* need her," Darren corrected bluntly. "You need a personality transplant."

Pratt sputtered, unable or unwilling to express his displeasure to this wealthiest of clients. Darren sighed and lifted a hand to the nape of his neck. For an instant Charly felt a stirring of *something* for him, sympathy, longing. Then, in the very same breath, she remembered the depth and breadth of his lies, the accusation against him. He had used her, for entertainment if nothing else. How it must have amused him. Why else would he have conducted a full-blown campaign to get to her? And she'd known it, blast him. She'd known it and allowed it, because she'd believed that he was good and kind and generous. She'd even allowed him to use her son. Why couldn't she use him then? Why shouldn't she? Suddenly she recalled that Pratt and a certain judge were very close friends. It bordered on unethical, but at the moment she couldn't seem to care.

Striking a nonchalant pose, she lifted her chin and looked at Pratt. "First, I want a raise, a sizable one."

Pratt muttered under his breath, but he nodded, glaring daggers at her and Darren, who still had not lifted his head. "Until I have the papers drawn up, Mr. Rudell is witness to my agreement to your terms."

"That's not all," Charly went on, her heart slamming painfully inside her chest. "You're friends with family court judge Stoner."

Pratt nodded and shrugged uncertainly. "We play golf together twice a week. Everyone knows that."

"I want you to speak to him," she said flatly, "about my adoption petition."

Darren looked up sharply. His gaze, when he turned it on Pratt was very pointed. Pratt swallowed and said, "I'll do better than that. I'll represent you at the hearing, if you want."

Slam dunk. With Pratt on her side, the adoption was a done deal. She'd never have dared ask under any other circumstances, knowing full well the payback a worm like Pratt would have expected. But the worm had turned in her favor.

She slung the strap of her handbag over one shoulder. "Tell Helen to call me at home. I'm taking the day off."

Pratt began sputtering objections, but Darren cut him off with a sharp wave of his hand. "I didn't do what she's accusing me of, Charly," he told her softly. "I won't say I didn't have an affair with her, but it was never more than mere sex, and even that was over before she moved into the empty apartment. I want you to know that."

"Yeah, right," she retorted. "That explains everything perfectly, *Mr. Rudell.*"

"Darling, I told you why I gave you a false name. I so desperately wanted a chance with you. Please tell me I still have it."

She laughed. She couldn't help it. They'd never had a chance. His lies had seen to that. "You can burn your team jersey," she told him coldly, "and submit your formal resignation to the commissioner."

He winced and gulped. "All right, if that's what

you want. But, Charly, someday you have to let me explain everything.''

Pointing her chin at Richard Pratt, she said, ''Explain it to someone who cares.'' With that she swept out of the room.

No one who saw her striding purposefully from the building would have guessed that she was dying inside.

''But why isn't he?'' Ponce asked for the third or fourth time. They were sitting in the car, directly behind the bleachers on the sideline of the soccer field where the team was scheduled to play shortly.

Charly tamped down her impatience and said, ''He just isn't. He has…important stuff going on right now.'' She couldn't bring herself to say Darren's name, not yet, maybe never. She was having enough trouble just *thinking* of him as Darren Keith, better known as D. K., Rudell. At least he hadn't lied about his given name.

''Not more important than the team,'' Ponce argued, shaking his head. ''I know.''

Charly held on to the frayed edge of her composure with the steely grip of pure desperation. ''I realize he probably told you that, but—''

''He didn't tell me,'' Ponce insisted. ''I just know.''

Sighing, Charly rubbed her forehead. She'd nursed a faint but intractable headache for days. ''He isn't coming, Ponce. I'm sorry, but you just have to accept that D—he isn't going to be around anymore.''

Her son stared at her with doubtful, troubled eyes as if wondering why she couldn't see what was so obvious to him. Then, shaking his head, he got out of the car. Charly stared at his empty seat for several moments, feeling lost and frighteningly vulnerable.

It had been her idea to fight fire with fire. Tawny Beekman was obviously intent on trying this case in the court of public opinion, either in an attempt to hurt Darren personally or in hopes of forcing him to settle out of court by making a fair trial in this venue impossible. Earlier, the identity of Ms. Beekman's former roommate had been leaked to the press. The woman in question, whom neither Charly nor any other member of the firm had ever met by implicit design, had been only too glad to let the public know that she'd tossed out Tawny after catching her own boyfriend in bed with "the slut."

The story had run on the front pages of the Dallas paper two days ago and in the Fort Worth press the next. Today's press conference had been called to "clean the hands" of the firm and, by association, its client. Charly only wished that someone else could have been chosen for the public hand washing, but she knew that hers was a dual role, female figurehead and attack dog in a skirt. Today she would play the former to the hilt.

Stepping up to the microphone, she smiled and proceeded to thank the press for coming. She then read a statement, her hands trembling while cameras whirred and snapped. Her hair and cosmetics had been done by the top stylist in the area just for this occasion, so she knew that she was looking her absolute best, but the idea of appearing on the evening news gave her a serious case of the nerves. She would have to take special care to keep Ponce from seeing it.

After expressing formal concern for the tone of the press coverage to date, the statement went on to point out that their client, Mr. Rudell, had no part in setting the current press circus in motion. While he had nothing to hide, he naturally would have preferred that Ms. Beekman's unfounded claims pass unnoticed. After reading the statement, she took a few questions.

When asked, despite the formal statement, if Rudell had any hand in bringing the latest information on Ms. Beekman to the press, Charly stated categorically that he had not, which was flatly true since, after mentioning the roommate's name in passing, he had been neither consulted nor informed about what that information had put in process. When pressed as to whether or not the firm had a hand in the previous day's coverage, Charly indignantly stated that no member or employee of the firm had ever had contact of any sort with the plaintiff's ex-roommate, who had been featured so prominently in the press recently. That, too, was true on its face. It had been the friend of a brother of a driver employed by a car service often used by the firm who had dropped the dime on Tawny Beekman's ex-roomie.

Finally the question Charly and her team had been hoping for, in some form, surfaced. It was asked by an uncertain young woman with a reputation for getting her facts wrong, but it was asked in front of an avid throng of newshounds.

"What do these latest revelations have to do with Mr. Rudell's relationship to Ms. Beekman?"

Charly bowed her head to hide her smile and appeared to fumble for an answer. "Well...not that Mr. Rudell would agree to necessarily answer that question, you understand—he is not, as you may have discovered, the sort of gentleman to kiss and tell—one, nevertheless, must ask oneself why a gentleman with his resources would consent to 'set up as his de facto wife,' as Ms. Beekman contends, a woman who was caught only days before in, ah, physical congress with another man, that is, her own roommate's boyfriend."

A murmur of rueful speculation went around the room, even as several hands shot into the air. Her mission accomplished by having created as much doubt about Tawny Beekman's story as possible, Charly demurred to answer further questions, saying deprecatingly, "I'm afraid I've said quite enough, perhaps too much. I just find these allegations about my client absurd, since it's painfully obvious that at no time did he take himself out of circulation. Oh! There I go again. Please you must excuse me. Thank you again for coming."

The newspeople shouted questions even as she left the dais and exited the door behind it, but Charly merely tossed apologetic smiles over her shoulder as she made her escape. Out of sight of the reporters, all four of the partners met her to congratulate her on her performance. It was Pratt, however, who patted her on the shoulder and exclaimed proudly, "Girlie, I knew you had it in you to be a first-rate lawyer!" Charly rolled her eyes and kept on walking. "What?" he asked, Cartere groaning. "What'd I say?"

Someone was explaining the niceties of address to him, "girlie" being an unacceptable substitute for "Ms. Bellamy," a grown woman and first-rate attorney whether or not Pratt was sagacious enough to realize it before now. Shaking her head, Charly turned the corner and bumped into Darren. His arms closed about her before she could even register what had happened. A familiar electricity shot through her, but she didn't have to be struck by lightning twice to protect herself when storm clouds hovered overhead. Shrugging free of him, she quickly stepped back.

"What are you doing here?"

"I, um, have that list of names."

Charly blanched. It was a list of women with whom he'd been involved during the past year, the year, supposedly when he'd been keeping Tawny Beekman in an extravagant love nest, depriving her of her normal means of support as a matter of male pride. Charly walked around him, saying, "Just give it to my assistant."

"I wanted to see you."

Her feet stopped of their own foolish accord, but

she managed to keep firm command of her tongue. "I *don't* want to see you."

Ignoring that, he said softly, "You look great, but I prefer the real you."

She folded her arms and made a decided effort to rebuff the pronounced flare of delight his words evoked. "The plain me, you mean."

"No. The real you could never be plain. Your beauty shines from the inside out."

She fended off a spurt of pleasure with sarcasm. "I suppose I should say thank you for that. But I won't. Now if you'll excuse me..."

"How is Ponce?"

She rocked back on her heels. "You have some nerve asking that."

"I miss him. I hope he's not confused by all this."

"He knows nothing of all this."

He sighed with obvious relief. "That's good. But he must be wondering where I've gone. He's too smart not to. If you'd ever like me to speak to him about it, I'd be glad to."

"No! No, I would not like you to speak to him about it."

Darren lifted a hand to his forehead. "Maybe we should just settle," he muttered, "get this whole mess out of the way so we can—"

"Settle?" she echoed, derailing that thought before he could complete it. "Then you're admitting that you used Tawny Beekman?"

He shook his head listlessly. "No. I tried to help Tawny, nothing more. I didn't lead her on. I didn't make promises. I didn't sleep with her, not after she moved into the building and not even for a while before. But what difference does it make?" He lifted a perfectly agonized gaze to hers. "What difference does it make now?"

She knew very well what he was asking for, and some part of her wanted to give him a reason to keep fighting, but she couldn't bring herself to do it. After all, he was very likely guilty of everything Tawny Beekman accused him of, not that she truly considered the Beekman woman a victim, not anymore. Nevertheless, he would be wiser to settle, especially considering what the firm was charging him for their services. It was not, however, her problem, and she would not allow herself to become personally involved. So she kept her personal opinions to herself and merely walked away, the lawyer in her retorting evenly, "That's up to you. I expect to get paid, either way."

Employing a greater force of will than should have been necessary, she managed not to look back.

He simply could not believe how much it hurt. Watching Charly walk away knowing that she detested him was like receiving a death sentence. His life as he had come to envision it was over, and somehow he couldn't seem to even imagine another.

He couldn't reach her, couldn't make her understand that she and Ponce were everything to him now. For the first time in his life he didn't know what to do, what to say, how to stop the pain. Oh, he had money all right, but without Charly and Ponce what did it matter? What had it ever mattered?

Oh, God, what a fool he had been. Was. Always would be now.

Chapter Ten

Looking again at the subpoena delivered to their office the day before, the very day after they'd agreed to a prearbitration meeting, Charly muttered, "Why would they want a video surveillance tape?"

Helen shook her head. "Beats me. One thing's for sure, though, that woman's got more tricks than a traveling magic show." Helen parked herself on the corner of Charly's desk and told her what their investigator had found out. "Our guy nosed around the joint where Beekman dances—and I use the term *very* loosely. The story is that she performed there without pay because Rudell got a charge out of it."

"I find that hard to believe," Charly said, unable to reconcile that thought with the Darren she knew, or had thought she knew.

"So does our investigator," Helen said. "He couldn't find any actual evidence that Rudell was ever at that club. Tawny herself admits that they met at a party. He says that he realized what she did for a living at about the same time she was booted out by her roommate, and that he finds it distasteful. She says he was turned on by it, but nobody could give our guy any specific dates when Rudell supposedly attended performances. They couldn't offer receipts, names of anyone who came in with him, nothing. And Rudell's limo driver didn't even know where the place was."

Charly laid aside the paper she'd been studying and rose to her feet. "Okay, we won't worry about her contention that he deprived her of her liveli-hood. This video thing worries me, though. I can't believe Da—Mr. Rudell doesn't know what's going on there."

Helen didn't have to point out that if Charly had questioned her client about this herself, she might not have these doubts "All he could think of," Helen told her, "is a brief argument they had in the elevator bay."

"There must be more to it," Charly said. "Let's take a look."

Though it was late and she'd only managed a quick dinner with Ponce, who was at home in the company of his great-grandmother, she really had no choice but to study the tape immediately. A meeting had been arranged for the next morning by Beekman's side in an obvious attempt to force a settlement. Both sides were supposed to lay their cards on the table, a minitrial, so to speak, each side hoping to prove to the other that they couldn't win in court. Charly had gone along with the stratagem, intending to blow Beekman out of the water early. Then Beekman's attorney had dropped a bomb at the last possible moment by requesting a copy of a certain surveillance tape from Darren's apartment building. Charly couldn't allow that bomb to detonate.

Helen got up and withdrew two tapes from the bag she'd placed on a chair in front of Charly's desk. One of them was obviously a videotape. The other was significantly smaller. "Rudell said something about the audio being separate," Helen told her offhandedly, "so I figured I might as well get that one, too, just in case."

Charly nodded as she picked up the videotape and headed toward the screening room. The audio accompaniment remained, for the time being, on the desk blotter, a testament to Helen's laudable attention to detail. It was only later, after viewing the video, that either of them even remembered it.

At first, Charly couldn't believe what she saw on the videotape. Then she feared that Darren Rudell had duped her far more seriously than she'd understood. It was sheer desperation that prompted Helen to retrieve the audio recording from Charly's desk and insist they listen to it. Sick at heart, Charly agreed. Afterward, she knew exactly what to do.

Charly shrugged at the partners and said for the third time in as many minutes, "But we don't need them."

Dennis Cartere was the only who hadn't argued that the two women standing apart at the opposite end of the long room ought to stay and give their statements. He seemed no more able to keep his gaze off the shapely, high-heeled, long-haired duo than the others, however. Darren, on the other hand, stood alone with his friend and personal lawyer, Walt Anselm, gazing out the window.

Charly knew that after what she'd seen and *heard* the night before, she probably should have called all four of the partners at home, but the lateness of the hour and the work to be done had decided her against it. The clock on her bedside table had read eight minutes after four o'clock in the morning when she'd finally kicked off her shoes. With less than three hours' sleep she'd barely managed to shower, dress and get to the meeting on time, at a large conference room in her own firm's building. Beekman's side appeared to be running a bit later, however.

"It's absurd to think we don't need their testimony," Pratt said. As he spoke, he smiled and nodded at a very tall, leggy brunette with a wealth of curly hair.

Charly refrained, barely, from rolling her eyes. "I'm telling you that I have all the ammunition we need to put Ms. Tawny Beekman out of the extortion business."

The female in question entered the room just then with her attorney, a fortyish, well-tailored gentleman. A stenographer and two strange men followed. One of whom wore an expensive Italian suit, slicked-back hair and a cocky grin, while the other, obviously the older of the two, sported a poorly fitting jacket in a loud plaid and a look of distinct unease.

"Load your guns, Counselor," Dennis Cartere murmured to Charly. "The battle officially begins."

"And in case your shot's not as powerful as you think," Pratt said, "we'll send in the infantry first."

Charly brought her hands to her hips in pure disgust. Begrudgingly, she led the way to the long, narrow conference table positioned in the center of the room. After greeting Ms. Beekman's attorney, Johnson Ward, and then Ms. Beekman herself, Charly had Helen send in their own stenographer, who would be making their own record of the proceedings. When everyone had been introduced, Charly sent the witnesses out of the room and got down to business.

"This meeting has been called in a good-faith effort to put this suit to rest," she said. "While witnesses are not being sworn, they will be expected to sign as statements transcripts of their testimony here. We will use an informal debate platform. In all fairness, however, I think I should tell plaintiff and her attorney now that we possess clear and irrefutable evidence of her intention to extort money from our client."

"Fat chance," Tawny Beekman snorted. She threw a venomous glare at Darren and added, "In fact, if he doesn't want to be charged with assault, he'd better settle quick."

"Assault!" Darren yelped, as Beekman's attorney quieted her with a hand on her wrist. Walt Anselm leaned over and whispered in Darren's ear. Nodding, Darren subsided, but the glance he shot at Charly stated emphatically what she already knew.

"Perhaps *I* should warn *you*," Beekman's attorney said to Charly, "that we believe we have irrefutable proof of your client's abuse of Ms. Beekman. At any rate, we intend to make our case."

Charly sighed. "If you insist on playing out this farce, so be it. How do you want to proceed?"

"We'll hear first from Mr. Londel," Ward said.

Londel, the owner of a so-called gentleman's club, was called in and proceeded to lie like a rug on the hearth. According to him, he hadn't paid Tawny to dance in a year, ever since she "moved in with Rudell." He continued to schedule her appearances, he said, because she wanted to please her boyfriend, namely Darren, who apparently got a major charge out of her dancing.

The other defense witness was far more nervous than Londel but did, nevertheless, disgorge the lie expected of him. According to him, Tawny danced because Darren wanted her to, and Darren had bragged about her doing it for free because he took pride in being able to support "his woman."

"I never said any such thing!" Darren vowed. "I've never even seen this man before in my life."

Some verbal wrangling followed, with Tawny and Darren calling each other liars. Charly was oddly pleased to see Darren in fighting form. In this, at least, he had not lied to her. Might he have been telling the truth about other things, as well? Pratt called their first witness to the table, a perfectly stunning model with long, straight, pale-blond hair and ice-blue eyes. Every guy in the room practically drooled. Except Darren, Charly noted with some satisfaction. Even Anselm, his attorney, couldn't seem to help smiling warmly at the woman, whose unlikely name was Morgana Hunter.

Ms. Hunter calmly and coolly testified that she had very publicly dated Mr. Rudell for several weeks earlier that year and that when they'd bumped into Ms. Beekman one evening Ms. Beekman herself had stated that she and Mr. Rudell were "neighbors and friends." Tawny denied it, of course, and claimed that the dating was all for show, that she allowed it because Darren convinced her that his reputation as a playboy was important for his business as it kept his name in the papers. Darren just rolled his eyes, and the next witness was called.

Rita Carpenter, an actress prominent on the local theater scene, testified in much the same manner as Morgana Hunter, except she stated bluntly that she once considered moving into Darren's plush apartment building only to be told in no uncertain terms by him that it would be the end of their "friendship." It was apparent, she said, that Darren tried to protect himself by refusing to carry on a personal relationship with anyone who got too close.

"We all knew that Darren wasn't ready for personal commitment,'' she said, ''and that when he was, he wouldn't fool around about it.''

Darren turned his head just then and looked at Charly. Was it possible that he hadn't merely set out to seduce her? Could it have been more than that all along? He hadn't, after all, warned her that it could be nothing more than fun and games between them as he had these other women. He had, in fact, said that he loved her and wanted to marry her, although his timing in that could have been better. What was he thinking, feeling now? She had rejected him, been colder to him than anyone else in her memory. What if he was sincere? Charly couldn't help wondering if she was as stupid in her own way as Tawny Beekman was in hers.

She put away her personal concerns, however, the instant the plaintiff's attorney produced the video. Tawny no doubt believed that the tape was the clincher, that Darren would surely agree to settle once the thing was shown. Charly, however, knew that it would be Tawny's downfall. She said nothing as the tape was played, showing Beekman coming on to Darren in the elevator nook, the heated exchange that followed and Tawny following Darren as he walked away, out of sight of the camera. Johnson fast forwarded the tape through what he called ''several moments of dead time.'' Then Tawny staggered back into view on the screen, her hair mussed, bodice torn and throat bruised, and Johnson Ward paused the tape there for dramatic effect.

"I think that speaks for itself," Ward announced smugly.

Looking directly at Charly, Darren exclaimed, "That isn't what it seems. I didn't do that to her!"

"The camera doesn't lie!" Tawny refuted.

"But it doesn't always tell the whole story, either," Charly stated calmly. With that, she placed the audio tape on the table. Helen immediately got up and began passing out copies of the statement signed by Darren's head of security at the apartment building.

"The security agent who made this recording," Charly stated, "told his superior that he did so because Mr. Rudell had seemed upset when Ms. Beekman came on the scene. He was concerned, he says, for Mr. Rudell's well-being because of the suspicion that Mr. Rudell's private elevator had been intentionally sabotaged."

Tawny laughed nervously at that and proclaimed loudly that no matter what was wrong with the elevator, the video proved Darren had assaulted her when she'd begged him not to throw her out in the street. Charly just smiled and moved to the video player with a tape of her own, one with the video and audio integrated. She'd spent hours putting it together the evening before, and while the quality was not as good as she'd have liked, it was good enough.

"Let's try this again," she said, pushing the play button. This time the chain of events started earlier.

The video showed Darren trying the elevator, then calling security. The audio, though not per-

fectly synchronized, was clearly audible, as was
every word spoken that morning by Darren and
Tawny. Even the sound of Tawny slapping Darren
came through with unmistakable clarity, as did her
blatant threats. By the time the screen showed
Tawny stumbling around the corner of the elevator
bay, disheveled and now clearly feigning that she'd
been assaulted, everyone in the room knew that
Darren was innocent of Tawny's charges. Tawny,
however, couldn't seem to believe that her cause
was lost.

"This is rigged up!" Tawny exclaimed desperately, while her lawyer sat with his head in his
hands. "The words don't even match the move-
ments of our mouths!"

"You have the security guard's statement,"
Charly said calmly. "We'll call him to testify personally in court, of course, and the two tapes will
be synchronized perfectly by a professional."
Charly looked directly at Tawny and went on. "We
don't know yet how you sabotaged the elevator, but
I've no doubt we can figure it out. You staged this
whole scene, knowing it would be recorded by the
camera. You didn't count on the audio recording,
however, or the competence of Mr. Rudell's security staff."

"I didn't know anything about this," Johnson
Ward interjected heatedly. "I knew the case was
probably unwinnable in court, and so I applied myself to getting a settlement, but I did not know it
was a setup."

Charly nodded. "I assume you'll be withdrawing your suit."

"Yes."

"No!" Tawny objected.

The lawyer addressed his client sternly. "Don't you get it? You'll be lucky if you aren't charged with attempted fraud and, I suspect, harassment. At the very least, you can expect Mr. Rudell to sue you for reimbursement of the money he's spent defending himself."

"If he'd have just given the money to me in the first place, I wouldn't have had to do it!" Tawny wailed. "He's got plenty!"

Johnson Ward sighed and addressed himself to Darren. "Please accept my apologies, Mr. Rudell. I really thought, I mean, given your reputation, that there was some substance to Ms. Beekman's claims."

Darren shook his head. "You're not to blame. My lifestyle would have given that same impression to anyone not in a position to know otherwise." His gaze went straight to Charly again. "I've made some positive changes in that area."

"That doesn't mean we won't be seeking restitution for legal expenses," Walter Anselm warned.

"Yes, it does," Darren contradicted. "It was never about the money."

"In that case," Charly said, pleased with this turn of events, "if Ms. Beekman makes a statement to the press that Darren is undeserving of the claims she's made against him, I'll recommend we forgo the extortion charges, as well."

Tawny paled at the suggestion of criminal charges. Johnson Ward got to his feet, saying, "If she doesn't make that statement, I will." Deflated, Tawny slumped forward. "The suit will be dropped tomorrow," he added, hauling her to her feet.

He dragged her from the room bawling, while the partners crowded around Darren congratulating him. Charly stood and looked around, feeling slightly disoriented and ragged with exhaustion. Knowing that she was anxious to get home to Ponce, Helen waved her toward the door with a congratulatory smile. Charly nodded, deciding that it was best to slip away while everyone else was otherwise occupied. She needed to sleep and then to think. She was almost out the door when she felt a hand on her shoulder and turned to look up into the face of Richard Pratt.

"Good job, Counselor."

His was not the face she had hoped to see, but in that quiet praise, she finally heard acceptance. "Thank you," she said, walking away.

Charly stretched and sleepily ruffled a hand through her hair as she walked through the quiet house in her pajamas. She'd been almost too tired to spend a few moments with Ponce and her grandmother before trundling off to bed for a nap. Three hours later she was feeling somewhat better. She could have slept much longer, but she had promised her son that they'd have lunch and the afternoon together. Charly's stomach rumbled in anticipation of the meal.

Lunch preparations, however, were not under way in the kitchen as expected, which was as deserted as the dining room, Ponce's bedroom and the family room when Charly trailed through them, yawning. When she wandered into the formal living room, however, she found someone waiting there.

He was sitting on the couch, elbows braced upon his knees, hands entwined patiently. Charly's heart thudded as he rose to his feet.

"Delphina and Ponce have gone to the grocery store. I didn't say anything to Ponce," he added quickly, "about what's been going on, I mean. It was good to see him, though." Darren rubbed his palms against his thighs, betraying a certain nervousness that she found endearing. "He seemed glad to see me."

"I imagine he was," she said, crossing her arms over her chest. The soft knit pajamas could not be called alluring or revealing by any stretch of the imagination, but they were sleepwear and as such brought the glaring notion of bed, and all that could transpire there, into the moment. Still, she didn't suggest that she ought to go change.

"Thank you for today," he said suddenly.

She shook her head. "Helen deserves more credit than I do. She's the one who came up with the audio tape. I think she said that you mentioned it."

He nodded. "I didn't really think anything of it, but when Helen brought up the video I remembered a conversation I'd had with a young couple in the elevator one day about possible audio taping. I never actually dreamed that a recording had been made of my argument with Tawny.''

''Good thing for you that it was.''

He smiled wanly. ''Yeah. That's not why I'm here, though.''

Charly could feel her heart beating. ''Why are you here?''

''Because I love you.''

Tears immediately welled in her eyes. ''Darren,'' she whispered, knowing she didn't want to fight her feelings any longer.

''Charly, I'd have told you,'' he said quickly. ''I swear to God, I was planning to tell you my real name when Tawny hit me with that stupid suit. I was planning, in fact, to buy a ring, confess all, and ask you to marry me.''

She was unaware that she was moving until she was within reach. ''Tell me again why you lied to me.''

He lifted his hands to her shoulders. ''I was afraid. I knew you'd run from a man like D. K. Rudell, and I was tired of him, Charly, so tired of him. I didn't realize how much. Deep inside, I wanted a chance to be different, and somehow I knew that you were my chance, maybe my only chance.''

''Why me?'' she asked. ''I'm not like those other women, Darren.''

''No, you're not,'' he said. ''You're real. Your beauty is real, everything about you is real. You're the best person I know, Charly, the sweetest, dearest, most conscientious. You're a good lawyer, Charly, a good mother. You'll be a good wife.''

"My first husband didn't think so.''

"That loser was outclassed, and he knew it, Charly. I suspect even you know it. I talked to Delphina. She says you settled for him because you wanted a family. I want a family, too, Charly, but I'm not willing to settle for anything but the best—whether I deserve it or not—and that's you.''

Charly bit her lip to keep from answering his crooked smile with one of her own. "I don't honestly know if I have time to be a good wife, Darren,'' she admitted. "My law practice is important. Maybe it doesn't bring in a lot of money, but that doesn't matter to me.''

"I know that, sweetheart. Believe it or not, it isn't particularly important to me, either, but it just so happens that I've managed to make a lot of it, and money does solve some problems. It can do a great deal of good in the right hands, and I'm thinking those hands belong to a certain crusading-lawyer-hot-shot-soccer-coach who already holds my heart. Texas *is* a community property state.''

Charly chuckled, tears rolling down her cheeks. "I know.''

He cupped her face. "Marry me, sweetheart. Give me a son and as many more kids as you want. Fight your good wars and champion every lost cause that comes our way. But, uh, leave the coaching to me. I think your talents are best used on the sidelines. You're the ultimate soccer mom, you know.''

She laughed and, blinking away the tears, quipped, ''How do you feel about T-ball?''

''I love T-ball,'' he said, putting his forehead to hers. ''How does our son feel about it?''

Our son.

She closed her eyes and said shakily, ''I do love you, Darren Keith Rudell.''

He slid his arms around her. ''Does that mean what I hope it means?''

She opened her eyes and speared him with a certain look. ''It means that I am going to rescue you from a wasted life of beautiful women, empty sex and outrageous behavior.''

He grinned. ''You have my eternal gratitude, Ms. Bellamy, or will have as soon as I can call you Mrs. Rudell.''

''Shut up and kiss me, you fool.''

He was doing just that and a very commendable job of it, too, when a cleared throat warned them that they were no longer alone. Charly turned within the warm confines of her future husband's arms to find her grandmother smiling and Ponce literally bouncing up and down.

''Well?'' he squeaked, raising his eyebrows at Darren. ''Did she say yes?''

''She did,'' Charly answered.

''So did I,'' he told her proudly.

''So did you?'' she responded in some confusion.

''Sure,'' he said, folding his arms in satisfaction, ''he asked me to marry him, too.''

Charly tilted her head back to look up at Darren. ''How else is a guy supposed to be sure he's

getting the whole package?'' he asked with a wink
and a shrug.

"Quite right,'' she said with mock severity as
Ponce ran toward them.

"We're gonna be a whole fam'ly now, aren't
we?'' he said, throwing his arms around their legs.
Darren stooped and lifted him up.

"We sure are,'' he said.

"We was a real fam'ly before,'' Ponce explained, "me and Mama and Granna Pheldina, but
now we're a *whole* one, isn't that so, Granna?''

"That's exactly right,'' Delphina said with a
pleased laugh.

"Whole and growing,'' Charly said, turning to
lay her head upon Darren's shoulder and take her
son's hand in her own. Darren bowed his head and
found her mouth with his. Her doubts—about all of
them—were forever put to rest, and her every
dream was finally coming true. Who would have
predicted that this wealthy playboy could fall in
love with the ultimate soccer mom? Her mind flew
back over that day she'd walked into Dave's shop
looking for a handout, and it occurred to her with
a large degree of mirthful wonder that she was actually kissing that brilliant person who had thought
up Retail Staff Appreciation Day, just as she'd
wanted to. And she always would.

*   *   *   *   *

MILLS & BOON®

Live the emotion

NOVEMBER 2003 HARDBACK TITLES

ROMANCE™

His Boardroom Mistress *Emma Darcy*   H5892   0 263 17787 4
The Blackmail Marriage *Penny Jordan*   H5893   0 263 17788 2
Their Secret Baby *Kate Walker*   H5894   0 263 17789 0
His Cinderella Mistress *Carole Mortimer*   H5895   0 263 17790 4
A Convenient Marriage *Maggie Cox*   H5896   0 263 17791 2
The Spaniard's Love-Child *Kim Lawrence*

   H5897   0 263 17792 0
His Inconvenient Wife *Melanie Milburne*   H5898   0 263 17793 9
The Man with the Money *Arlene James*   H5899   0 263 17794 7
The Frenchman's Bride *Rebecca Winters*   H5900   0 263 17795 5
Her Royal Baby *Marion Lennox*   H5901   0 263 17796 3
Her Playboy Challenge *Barbara Hannay*   H5902   0 263 17797 1
Mission: Marriage *Hannah Bernard*   H5903   0 263 17798 X
The Marriage Clause *Karen Rose Smith*   H5904   0 263 17799 8
A Little Moonlighting *Raye Morgan*   H5905   0 263 17800 5
The Pregnant Surgeon *Jennifer Taylor*   H5906   0 263 17801 3
The Registrar's Wedding Wish *Lucy Clark*

   H5907   0 263 17802 1

HISTORICAL ROMANCE™

The Unknown Wife *Mary Brendan*   H563   0 263 17839 0
A Damnable Rogue *Anne Herries*   H564   0 263 17840 4

MEDICAL ROMANCE™

Outback Marriage *Meredith Webber*   M481   0 263 17863 3
The Bush Doctor's Challenge *Carol Marinelli*

   M482   0 263 17864 1

MILLS & BOON®

Live the emotion

NOVEMBER 2003 LARGE PRINT TITLES

ROMANCE™

The Frenchman's Love-Child *Lynne Graham*

	1623	0 263 17947 8
One Night with the Sheikh *Penny Jordan*	1624	0 263 17948 6
The Borghese Bride *Sandra Marton*	1625	0 263 17949 4
The Alpha Male *Madeleine Ker*	1626	0 263 17950 8
Manhattan Merger *Rebecca Winters*	1627	0 263 17951 6
Contract Bride *Susan Fox*	1628	0 263 17952 4
The Blind-Date Proposal *Jessica Hart*	1629	0 263 17953 2
With This Baby... *Caroline Anderson*	1630	0 263 17954 0

HISTORICAL ROMANCE™

Wayward Widow *Nicola Cornick*	261	0 263 18007 7
My Lady's Dare *Gayle Wilson*	262	0 263 18008 5

MEDICAL ROMANCE™

To the Doctor: A Daughter *Marion Lennox*	485	0 263 18027 1
A Mother's Special Care *Jessica Matthews*	486	0 263 18028 X
Rescuing Dr MacAllister *Sarah Morgan*	487	0 263 18029 8
Dr Demetrius's Dilemma *Margaret Barker*	488	0 263 18030 1

MILLS & BOON®

Live the emotion

DECEMBER 2003 HARDBACK TITLES

ROMANCE™

Sold to the Sheikh *Miranda Lee*	H5908	0 263 17803 X
His Inherited Bride *Jacqueline Baird*	H5909	0 263 17804 8
The Bedroom Barter *Sara Craven*	H5910	0 263 17805 6
The Sicilian Surrender *Sandra Marton*	H5911	0 263 17806 4
McGillivray's Mistress *Anne McAllister*	H5912	0 263 17807 2
The Tycoon's Virgin Bride *Sandra Field*	H5913	0 263 17808 0
The Italian's Token Wife *Julia James*	H5914	0 263 17809 9
A Spanish Engagement *Kathryn Ross*	H5915	0 263 17810 2
Part-Time Fiancé *Leigh Michaels*	H5916	0 263 17811 0
Bride of Convenience *Susan Fox*	H5917	0 263 17812 9
Her Boss's Baby Plan *Jessica Hart*	H5918	0 263 17813 7
Assignment: Marriage *Jodi Dawson*	H5919	0 263 17814 5
In Deep Waters *Melissa McClone*	H5920	0 263 17815 3
Least Likely to Wed *Judy Christenberry*	H5921	0 263 17816 1
A Very Single Wife *Fiona McArthur*	H5922	0 263 17817 X
The Doctor's Family Secret *Joanna Neil*	H5923	0 263 17818 8

HISTORICAL ROMANCE™

The Viscount's Bride *Ann Elizabeth Cree*	H565	0 263 17841 2
Her Guardian Knight *Joanna Makepeace*	H566	0 263 17842 0

MEDICAL ROMANCE™

Outback Encounter *Meredith Webber*	M483	0 263 17865 X
The Nurse's Rescue *Alison Roberts*	M484	0 263 17866 8

MILLS & BOON®

Live the emotion

DECEMBER 2003 LARGE PRINT TITLES

ROMANCE™

At the Spaniard's Pleasure *Jacqueline Baird*

	1631	0 263 17955 9
Sinful Truths *Anne Mather*	1632	0 263 17956 7
His Forbidden Bride *Sara Craven*	1633	0 263 17957 5
Bride by Blackmail *Carole Mortimer*	1634	0 263 17958 3
Runaway Wife *Margaret Way*	1635	0 263 17959 1
The Tuscan Tycoon's Wife *Lucy Gordon*	1636	0 263 17960 5
The Billionaire Bid *Leigh Michaels*	1637	0 263 17961 3
A Parisian Proposition *Barbara Hannay*	1638	0 263 17962 1

HISTORICAL ROMANCE™

Beloved Virago *Anne Ashley*	263	0 263 18009 3
Rake's Reward *Joanna Maitland*	264	0 263 18010 7

MEDICAL ROMANCE™

The Surgeon's Second Chance *Meredith Webber*

	489	0 263 18031 X
Saving Dr Cooper *Jennifer Taylor*	490	0 263 18032 8
Emergency: Deception *Lucy Clark*	491	0 263 18033 6
The Pregnant Police Surgeon *Abigail Gordon*	492	0 263 18034 4